WHAT PEOPLE ARE SAYING ABOUT POKÉMON

"As advocates of activities that bring families together, we at *Child* magazine are thrilled to see a kid craze that crosses gender lines and appeals to preschoolers as well as preteens. Say 'yeah!' to **Pokémon**."
—*Sylvia Barsotti, executive editor,* Child

"There is a lesson in Pokémon for all of us: Kids are learninding enough p in-depth y not get fro nts and educa ind of motiv that the Pokémon phenomenon produces."
—*Irwin, N. Jankovic, Ph.D.,* Los Angeles Times

"For my family, **Pokémon** has resulted in many genuine one-on-one, Kodak-moment, fun connections with my kids and their friends— far more than I imagined I would enjoy. Being an effective parent is so much easier when we enjoy the same things our kids enjoy; when instead of doing something for them, we're doing something with them."
—Doug Hall and Russ Quaglia ("Two Dads" syndicated through Universal Press Syndicate), *Seattle Post Intelligencer*

"Pokémon presents teachers with a wonderful opportunity for character education. I suggest an integration of Pokémon in math, reading, spelling, language arts, music, and art. Students are already motivated."

—*Nathan Dearing, Teacher,* The Idaho Statesman

"If you listen closely to what your kids are talking about, you'll discover many valuable lessons in **Pokémon**. First and foremost, **Pokémon** breaks down social barriers. The shyest child only has to get a whiff of the trading cards to confront a strange kid and ask, 'Got cards?'"

—*Cynthia Tavlin, The Hackensack, NJ Record*

"Take into consideration the benefit Pokémon can have with a family that sits at the dinner table in silence night after night. Speaking to children in their language certainly breaks the ice."

—*Matthew W. Phelps*, The Providence Journal

The authors would like to acknowledge the following people, whose work was invaluable in the creation of this book: Glenn Elliott, Michael Gills, Robert Gutschera, David Noonan, Michael G. Ryan, and Tom Wylie.

Pokémon Made Simple

Design: Peter Whitley
First Printing: March 2000
Library of Congress Catalog Card Number: 00-100226

9 8 7 6 5 4 3 2 1

ISBN: 0-7869-1766-0

STOCK NUMBER-TSR21766

U.S., CANADA,
ASIA, PACIFIC, & LATIN AMERICA
Wizards of the Coast, Inc.
P.O. Box 707
Renton, WA 98057-0707
+1-800-324-6496

EUROPEAN HEADQUARTERS
Wizards of the Coast, Belgium
P.B. 2031
2600 Berchem
Belgium
+32-70-23-32-77

FOREWORD

• • • • • • • • • • • • • •

WHAT A DIFFERENCE A YEAR MAKES. A year ago I was asked to put together a special section for *Duelist* magazine on a new game called **Pokémon**. I had to ask, "What's **Pokémon** and why would our readers be interested in it?" Boy, was I about to get an education.

Not only did we produce a 12-page section for *Duelist* #35, but we also put Pikachu on the cover. That issue outsold every *Duelist* issue all the way back to issue #3. At the same time, the **Pokémon** phenomenon began to explode across North America and my own children (6-year-old Elyse and 4-year-olds Bryan and Ian) got caught up in the **Pokémon** wave.

It was time I learned more about **Pokémon**. My wife and I bought a Game Boy for each kid (hoping to ease our summer trip), but we ended up playing **Pokémon Blue** and **Pokémon Red** more than the kids. We helped each other defeat Gym Leaders, traded Pokémon through the link cable, and whiled away too many hours after the kids went to bed staring at that little 2-inch screen.

But that time paid off. My children and I have a special bond through **Pokémon**. We all get excited about opening booster packs when a new card set hits, and we all play the **Pokémon** trading card game (TCG). We watch the new episodes every Saturday morning, and I actually understand questions like, "What's good against Bulbasaur?"

In addition, when Wizards of the Coast launched *TopDeck* magazine to cover the **Pokémon** TCG and all our other trading card games, our publisher asked me to start writing "Pokémon for Parents"— advice for our Pokémon section. He realized that Pokémon parents need advice and that we could give it to them. So, in one year, I've gone from Pokémon novice to published expert. And I have my kids to thank for that (as well as Nintendo and Wizards of the Coast).

In this book, we try to share some of our collective expertise with both parents and kids caught up in the Pokémon phenomenon. The first section is a guide for parents who need help figuring out and handling this craze. In the second section, we teach you how to play the **Pokémon** TCG and give you some tips for playing the game and building better decks. Section three tells you all about the **Pokémon** TCG League and also gives you some trading and collecting tips.

Yes, it's been a wild year, but this trip isn't over yet. And if you're just getting on the Pokémon bus, welcome aboard. It's a fun ride.

WILL MCDERMOTT

EDITOR IN CHIEF, *TOPDECK* MAGAZINE

CONTENTS

● ● ● ● ● ● ● ● ● ● ● ● ●

· · · · · · · · · · · · · · · · · · ·

PARENTS GUIDE
TO POKÉMON

WELCOME TO THE
WORLD OF POKÉMON

POKÉMON. IT'S A WORD THAT PROBABLY strikes terror into your heart even now. But it's too late. If you are reading this book it means that either you or your child has gotten caught up in the biggest craze ever to hit North America (and probably the world): **Pokémon**.

This book is our attempt to help you make sense of it all and to get you up to speed on this amazing phenomenon so you can talk to your kids without being baffled by words like *Bulbasaur*, *Mewtwo*, and *Pikachu*. Through it all, we'll keep coming back to one rule: You set the limits on this phenomenon—

not your child and not some big corporation—you!

But to do that, you have to understand it.

SO, WHAT IS POKÉMON, ANYWAY?

Pokémon is short for **Pocket Monsters**, which is the name given to this game and phenomenon in Japan, where it all started. **Pokémon** began as a computer game world where humans live side-by-side with creatures called Pokémon. In the game, you can catch these creatures, train them, and battle with them against other trainers in an attempt to become the greatest Pokémon Master ever.

But **Pokémon** is just that—a game. And it is a computer game with no blood or gore, which is kind of refreshing today. In fact, the Pokémon never die, they just faint when they get tired or injured (in the TCG, they get Knocked Out). There are even special places in the game called Pokémon Centers where you can heal your Pokémon for free.

Pokémon came from the mind of game developer Satoshi Tajiri. With the help of Tsunekazu Ishihara (who currently directs all the **Pokémon** properties), Tajiri and others at his GameFreak software company brought the 151 pocket monsters to life in a com-

TRIVIA
The **Pokémon** TCG is based on a Nintendo GameBoy game that was first released in Japan.

plex world that fits inside a Nintendo Game Boy game.

But that was just the first step on the path to the commercial success that **Pokémon** has become. In 1996 Nintendo released the **Pocket Monsters** Game Boy cartridges (Red and Green) in Japan. These took the Japanese market by storm, selling 4 million copies and breaking sales records. Shortly afterwards the animated series debuted, which kept the game hot and opened up other merchandising opportunities, including the **Pocket Monsters** trading card game.

That was 1997.

Flash forward to today. **Pokémon** has become a worldwide phenomenon that has grossed more than $5 billion in just four years (more than *Star Wars*, which has been around for 25 years). Leading the charge in the United States is the **Pokémon** trading card game, which is produced and distributed in North America by Wizards of the Coast, makers of the original trading card game, **Magic: The Gathering** (more about what a trading card game is later).

Since **Pokémon** made the jump across the Pacific, all the elements that made it hugely popular in Japan have been established in North America. These include:

● **Pokémon Red, Pokémon Blue, and Pokémon Yellow Game Boy cartridge**s. These games are fun and easy for kids as young as four. Plus they encourage kids to play (and trade) together, which gets more than one child involved at a time.

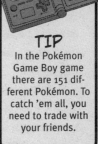

● **Pokémon Trading Card Game**. Again, this is a fun and easy game, but with cards that kids love to collect and trade. They are the baseball cards of a new generation.

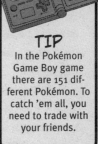

TIP

In the Pokémon Game Boy game there are 151 different Pokémon. To catch 'em all, you need to trade with your friends.

● **Pokémon Animated Series**. This is truly the glue that binds it all together. The series shows kids a world where children are confident and independent, can venture out alone, and have some control over their own lives as well as the lives of other creatures.

● **Pokémon toys, clothes, and other licensed merchandise**. These are the inevitable products of a successful property. As the Pokémon phenomenon grows, we'll see more and more of these.

● *Pokémon: The First Movie*. This blockbuster animated movie blew away records set by the king of animation, Walt Disney. The movie definitely showed the power of Pikachu (and the power of the trading card game cards used by the Kids WB! Network to promote the movie).

WHY IS POKÉMON SO POPULAR?

So, why is **Pokémon** so popular? First of all, **Pokémon** provides both cute creatures for girls (Pikachu, for example) and more fearsome monsters for boys (like Charizard, the fire-breathing lizard). Plus **Pokémon** taps into two very basic needs for children ages 6 to 12: collecting and playing games.

Whether it's stamps, coins, marbles, or **Pokémon** TCG cards, kids love to collect things. This is one of the reasons why the "gotta catch 'em all" message is so powerful. Collecting is actually a very large part of establishing an identity for a child. By collecting things, children say who they are. And when their friends collect the same things, a child gets to say that he or she is part of the group.

In addition, kids love to play games. The grade school years are an important time for them to learn about competition. This will be a big part of their lives, so children must understand early on that there are rules you need to learn and follow when you compete. And this goes beyond just the rules of the game. Learning how to play fair and how to lose gracefully are just as important, if not more so.

The **Pokémon** games satisfy all of these interests. The trading card game in particular blends collecting, playing, and socializing. Kids collect the **Pokémon** cards, trade with their friends (which helps build social skills), and learn to play a game that requires reading, math, and decision-making skills.

These are all very positive forces in your child's life that can help your child mature. If your child is just starting to read, add, and subtract (or needs help in any of these areas), **Pokémon** can provide both the incentive and the practice he or she needs to master these skills. If your child needs a way to connect with schoolmates, **Pokémon** cards are the perfect icebreaker for the school age set.

Your job as a parent is to help your kids learn the tough lessons, like "it's okay to lose as long as you did your best," to guide them through the pitfalls, and to protect them from the dangers inherent in any huge commercial phenomenon. Through it all, we firmly believe that both you and your children will get more out of your Pokémon experience if you experience it together.

BENEFITS OF POKÉMON

We know you will probably take this section with a grain of salt since this book comes to you from the same company that produces the **Pokémon** trading card game in the United States. Some of us are **Pokémon** parents and have kids caught up in the Pokémon

FACT
Collecting and playing games are two things that nearly all kids love to do!

phenomenon, and even we were skeptical about the games (and the animated series) at first.

But a funny thing happened. After buying the Game Boy games for our kids, we ended up playing them more than the kids did. We played the trading card game and found we liked it and that our kids liked playing **Pokémon** against us (because they could beat us, we suspect). Those of us with school-age children even started watching the animated series with our kids, and found we enjoyed it.

The point we're trying to make here is that **Pokémon** has become, for us, something that we do *with* our kids, not something we do *for* our kids.

We play the **Pokémon** trading card game like our families used to play Uno or Go Fish. Will's two boys ask, "What's good against Bulbasaur?" Since he found he really enjoyed playing **Pokémon** Blue, he knows the answer. And the boys think that's pretty cool.

We'll talk more about this later when we get into "How to Manage the Phenomenon in Your House," but we think there's an important distinction between **Pokémon** and other fads like Furby or Power Rangers: The Game Boy and the TCG are both games, not toys.

SKILL DEVELOPMENT

To play the **Pokémon** TCG, kids need to do three things well. They need to be able to read the cards.

They need to be able to do simple math (addition and subtraction). And they need to be able to make some fairly complex decisions.

Unlike other card games, a trading card game has most of the rules of the game written right on the cards. Sure, there are rules that govern how you use the cards, but when it comes to playing the cards, you have to read them to figure out what you can do with them. So, as kids are playing **Pokémon**, they are practicing their reading without even realizing it.

FACT
The **Pokémon** TCG requires addition and subtraction skills, so kids practice these skills while playing.

In addition to the words, there are also several numbers on **Pokémon** cards. The most important numbers are the Hit Points and the attack damage of the Pokémon. Without going into the rules (we'll do that in the "Learn to Play Like a Master" section), when kids play the **Pokémon** TCG, they must add damage to the battling Pokémon and compare the total damage to the Pokémon's Hit Points. Once the total damage equals a Pokémon's Hit Points, that Pokémon gets Knocked Out. This requires kids to constantly add and subtract numbers while playing.

As a Pokémon gets close to being Knocked Out, players also have to make decisions like, "Should I remove this Pokémon from battle so it doesn't get

Evolution Stage & Name

This Basic Pokémon is called Pikachu, but we bet you already knew that.

Hit Points & Type

Pikachu can receive 40 points of damage before it's Knocked Out. The lightning symbol indicates that it's a Lightning Pokémon.

Basic Pokémon
Pikachu

40 HP

Mouse Pokémon, Length: 1' 4", Weight: 13 lbs.

Gnaw 10

Thunder Jolt Flip a coin. If tails, Pikachu does 10 damage to itself. 30

weakness   resistance   retreat cost

When several of these Pokémon gather, their electricity can cause lightning storms. LV. 12 #25

Illus. Mitsuhiro Arita

Attack Names

Pikachu can Gnaw and create a Thunder Jolt.

Attack Damages

Pikachu can Gnaw your opponent's Pokémon for 10 points of damage, or Thunder Jolt for 30.

Knocked Out or should I attack one more time?" Players in a **Pokémon** TCG game have to look ahead several turns while playing to try to figure out what their opponent is likely to do and how long they can continue pursuing their current tactics.

You don't always know what's in your opponent's hand of cards when playing **Pokémon**, so you need to make educated guesses about what your opponent can do based on his or her strategy so far. This is why trading card games have been compared to chess. They are strategic games that make you think about possible outcomes based on limited information.

THE IMPORTANCE OF RULES

As your child learns to play the **Pokémon** TCG, he or she is also learning something about the importance of rules. This is true of any game learned at an early age. For example, Will's daughter likes to "bend" the rules when they play games like checkers or Uno. She'll take an extra turn and say "I can do that." Will, on the other hand, is trying to teach her that she needs to follow the rules (while at the same time making sure she still enjoys the game). This is tough, but it's a natural part of

FACT
Every game of **Pokémon** will present multiple outcomes at each turn. In this way, the game is similar to chess, checkers, or Uno.

growing up.

Learning rules is an important step in a child's development. Children have to follow rules in team and individual sports. They also have to follow rules in school and at home (unless you enjoy complete chaos in your house and school). **Pokémon** (and really any other leisure game) is a great, nonthreatening way to help children understand this concept. Of course, to help your children play by the rules you need to learn them yourself.

POKÉMON IS SOCIAL

By its very nature, **Pokémon** is a social activity. The **Pokémon** trading card game requires you to find someone to play with. Plus, the "gotta catch 'em all" mantra makes kids search out other Pokémaniacs so they can trade cards in their search to complete their collections.

Pokémon gives kids their own vocabulary they can speak on the playgrounds, and in the parks, and in their own family rooms. It also gives them a reason to come together in the first place. Learning how to make friends and how to treat friends is incredibly important to a child's development. And they won't learn those skills by watching television or playing video games, but they can learn them by playing **Pokémon**.

THE DARKER SIDE

Unfortunately, **Pokémon** isn't all fun and games. **Pokémon** is a hugely popular set of products, and like any successful commercial venture, some people will try to take advantage of it and some people will become obsessed by it. You as a parent have to watch out for your kids to keep them safe as they venture into the world of Pokémon.

TIP
Kids can become fixated on collecting. As a parent, you should monitor their involvement to insure things don't get out of hand.

Let's talk first about obsessive behavior. Obsessive behavior can be a problem with any fad, and it can actually hit adults as easily as it can kids (ask some folks who got a little too caught up in Beanie Babies). Some of the possible problems you might encounter if you or your child get obsessed with **Pokémon** are spending too much money, forgetting about doing homework, not concentrating on important matters like school or work, or even violent outbursts.

You should watch for the following signs in yourself and in your children:

- bills going unpaid even though you can find money to buy more cards
- grades dropping or homework going unfinished even though your child can find time to play **Pokémon** every day
- fights erupting over **Pokémon** games or trades

THIEVES AND OPPORTUNISTS

Whenever you deal with a collectible, you are going to encounter thieves and opportunists who will bend or break the laws to make a buck. Unfortunately, the **Pokémon** TCG is no different. Let's face it, some cards are being bought and sold by collectors for large amounts of money. Where there is money to be made, there will be thieves trying to take it.

In addition to the thieves, though, are the opportunists. Some use their knowledge of the value, of the cards to con little kids out of their best cards so they can turn around and sell them to collectors.

In today's world, kids have to grow up pretty fast (perhaps too fast). Just as you need to teach your children to look both ways before they cross the road, you must teach them to watch their cards when they are out in public (whether at school, at a friend's house, or in a store). You also need to make sure you and your children understand the value of the cards, so you don't get taken by someone out to make a quick buck. We discuss how to make a good trade in the "Catching 'Em All" chapter later in this book.

COUNTERFEITING

Counterfeiters are a special category of opportunists. Counterfeit **Pokémon** TCG cards, toys, and clothing have already been seen and confiscated in

North America. Wizards of the Coast and Nintendo are working very hard to combat these counterfeits. For some help telling the difference between counterfeit and real **Pokémon** cards, read the "Frequently Asked Questions" chapter.

MANAGING THE PHENOMENON IN YOUR HOUSE

As we said earlier, the first step you must take in managing the Pokémon phenomenon is understanding it. There are several things you can and should do. First, learn how to play the game. This will be very rewarding because it will give you an activity you can do with your children. Plus, by understanding the game, you will be better able to judge whether your kids are spending too much time on it and whether they are getting fair trades for their cards.

Second, learn the language of Pokémon. Watching the animated series can help you learn the characters' names and how they interact in the story. You also need to learn the names of the Pokémon. There is a checklist of **Pokémon** TCG cards in the back of this book. That's a good place to start. Once you know these names, your children's vocabulary will become

TIP
Learning and getting comfortable with the **Pokémon** TCG should be your first step in understanding your kid's interest.

more recognizable.

Third, you need to learn the nuances of trading (like how to tell card rarities and how to tell the difference between a 1st Edition card and an unlimited card). Look at the sections on trading cards in the "Catching 'Em All" chapter for the answers to these questions. Then you might want to take a look at the "Ground Rules for Trading" chapter for some ideas on how to keep your kids safe from opportunists.

PLACING LIMITS

Children need to know their limits. In fact, most children will test the boundaries of those limits on a daily basis. It's not enough to set the limits. You have to follow through. If *you* break the rules by buying some more cards, your child will realize that the boundaries have changed and will try to push them outward.

So, try to set reasonable limits that you are comfortable with. If you set the limit too high, you will break your bank trying to keep up, because your kid will push you to the edge every time. If you set the limit too low, you will be tempted to break the boundaries yourself, which will mean you have no limits at all.

We can't tell you what your boundaries are. Perhaps you want to limit your children to only what they can buy with their own money. This will force them to learn a lot about the value of a dollar, but may be too limiting if they can't afford a lot of cards (which may cause you to break the limits too often). Or you can set a dollar limit on the number of cards you will purchase for them on a regular basis and let them know that if they want more cards they have to earn them.

TIP
Learning the trading values of the different **Pokémon** cards will help you and your child make fair trades.

There are ways you can break the boundaries and not get yourself in trouble. In fact, you can use **Pokémon** to modify your child's behavior by rewarding them for behavior that you want to reinforce or change.

Many parents use **Pokémon** TCG cards to reward their children for doing homework, getting good grades, or working around the house. Rewards have been a part of parenting for a long time. Most of us used to get an allowance for chores done around the house and extra money for good grades. You may call this bribery, but it's really just positive reinforcement. Just as you punish your child for bad behavior, you need to reward your child for good behavior. In fact, some child experts say you need to praise a child 10 times for every behavior you want to reinforce.

The secondary benefit of establishing a reward system is that your kids get your attention when

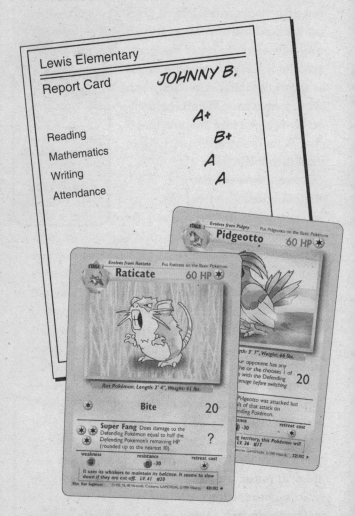

Lewis Elementary

Report Card

JOHNNY B.

Reading *A+*

Mathematics *B+*

Writing *A*

Attendance *A*

Pokémon Rewards

Good behavior can be reinforced with fun cards.

you give them the reward. So, think about how you can incorporate **Pokémon** TCG cards into your reward system at home. Perhaps cards can be part of their weekly allowance. You can offer them a booster pack of cards for every "A" they bring home from school. Whatever system you adopt, just make sure you stick to it.

DEALING WITH LIMITS

The problem with limits is that different parents will have different boundaries, so your child may fall behind in the race to "catch 'em all." A lot of peer pressure exists even in grade school and, unfortunately, popularity can be tied to how much stuff you have. So, you will have to be prepared to deal with your child's need to keep up with the Joneses.

Your natural tendency may be to give in so your kid can have just as many cards as their friends. But this will likely break your limits (and may break your checking account). There are other alternatives. For example, you can take the opportunity to teach your child about the free market system by making them earn extra money (even if it's from you) that they can use to buy more cards. If your kids

TIP
Some child experts say that a parent should praise a child ten times a day for every good deed.

are willing, give them extra chores to do every week to earn more money for cards.

The other alternative is to teach your children how to make do with what they have. Say your child plays the game and wants to build a deck just like a friend has. But that deck has a lot of rare cards that your child doesn't have. That's okay. You can often substitute other **Pokémon** cards for the ones they really want.

For example, Pinsir is a really good rare Pokémon from the *Jungle* set that a lot of kids like to use in Grass decks. If you don't have enough Pinsirs, you can look through the cards in your child's collection to find a substitute. You may find you have plenty of Tangelas because it is a common Grass **Pokémon** from the Base Set. Tangela isn't quite as good as Pinsir, but it is very close. So, your

Substitutes

You can use common cards in place of hard to find ones when you first start building decks.

child can use Tangela until he or she can trade for some more Pinsirs. You don't always have to use rare cards.

Of course, to help your child make these kinds of decisions, you really need to know how to play the game. So in the next chapter we'll help you learn the game. We'll give you some hints for figuring out the rules and tell you about some tools to help you learn those rules.

TIP
If your kids want more cards, you can take the opportunity to have them earn the cards by doing chores or helping out with something.

ENJOYING POKÉMON
WITH YOUR KIDS

WE MENTIONED IN THE LAST CHAPTER how important we think it is for parents to play **Pokémon** with their kids. Playing **Pokémon** is quality time you can spend with your kids away from the television or the computer. It engages your child's mind and allows you to interact in an activity they enjoy. You might find you enjoy it as well.

Of course, the **Pokémon** trading card game isn't War or Go Fish and the rules may seem daunting at first (although most kids pick it up very quickly). What we hope to do in this chapter is lay the groundwork so you can pick up the rules a little easier when you try to learn how to play, and give you access to some tools that can help you learn.

WHAT IS A TRADING CARD GAME?

The main difference between a TCG and a regular card game is that each player uses his or her own deck of cards when playing and these decks can be quite different from each other. So instead of having a common deck that both players draw from like you would when you play Hearts or Gin, both players draw cards from their own unique deck.

In the **Pokémon** trading card game, each player's deck can be different from every other player's deck because there are over 200 different cards you can put into a deck. That's part of the challenge and part of the fun. You have to figure out what your opponent is playing by watching how he or she plays.

The other difference between a TCG and other games is that kids trade these cards to each other (like baseball cards). Some kids try to complete a collection, others just want to get their favorite Pokémon, and the kids who play the game are always looking for just the right card for their latest deck (because many kids like to build their own decks).

So, between trading cards, building decks, and playing a game where each deck you face will be different from the last, you can see there is a lot more going on in a

FACT
In the **Pokémon** trading card game players make their own deck to bring to the match.

TCG than in a game like Hearts. The main thing to concentrate on is not the different cards, but the rules of the game itself, which are actually quite simple.

It is the differences in the cards that make a trading card game complex, because each one can bend the rules a little. But if you understand the basic rules of the game, it's easy enough just to read each new card as it is played and figure out how it works within the existing rules.

GETTING STARTED

The best way to learn the basic rules for the **Pokémon** trading card game is to use the **Pokémon** Starter Game set. This set uses two 30-card decks and walks you step-by-step through a short sample game. Some of these even come with an instructional videotape or a demo CD. So you can use the rulebook, your VCR, or your computer to help you learn how to play.

In those decks you will find three basic types of cards: Pokémon, Energy cards, and Trainer cards. The Pokémon are the creatures you send into battle. The Energy cards are how you power up your Pokémon for battle. The Trainer cards allow you to do many things like reduce the damage your Pokémon takes in battle, heal your Pokémon after a battle, and draw extra cards from your deck.

We'll go into more detail about how each of these

cards works in the "Learn to Play Like a Master" section. For now we'll concentrate on just the very basics. At its core, **Pokémon** is a strategic battle between you and your opponent. You move your pieces (the cards) into position to attack and try to take out your opponent's pieces while keeping your pieces safe.

Unlike chess or checkers, you don't have to move your pieces all over the board to take out your opponent's pieces. There are really only two "spaces" on a **Pokémon** "board": The Arena (where the Pokémon battle) and the Bench (where Pokémon rest between battles). In a way, it's like basketball. Your Active Pokémon is on the court trying to score while its teammates are on the Bench resting up for their turn.

Pokémon really is very much like a sport and you are the coach (or trainer, in this case). So, in a nutshell, all you do in the **Pokémon** TCG is put a Pokémon into the Arena, put some other Pokémon on your Bench in case that first Pokémon gets Knocked Out, use Energy cards to power up your Pokémon, and then try to Knock Out your opponent's Pokémon.

There are rules to follow for doing all these

> **TIP**
>
> Even though each different type of Pokémon is unique, once you understand the basic rules of the game it's easy to see how that Pokémon will be played.

things, but everything else you need to know to play the game is written on the cards. To learn the rules and to figure out how to read the cards, take a look at the "Let's Play **Pokémon**" chapter.

TOOLS TO HELP YOU LEARN POKÉMON

All of these items can help you learn to play:

- **Starter Video**. The starter videotape can walk you through your first game step-by-step and teach you all the rules you need to know to get started.

- **CD-ROM Demo**. The demo can guide you through the rules and even lets you play the game against a pretty good computer opponent to practice what you learn.

- Online Demo. In addition to the demo packaged in the Starter Gift Box, Wizards of the Coast provides an online demo at its Pokémon TCG website (www.wizards.com/Pokemon). This demo doesn't allow you to actually play the game, but it does take you visually through the basics of the game.

- **Playmat**. You can get **Pokémon** playmats from a lot of places, including most **Pokémon** TCG League centers. Playmats are helpful because they show you where to put your cards.

- **Pokémon TCG League centers**. The **Pokémon** TCG League is run in stores across North America. The Gym Leaders (the people who are trained to run the Leagues in these stores) should be able to teach you the game.

WHERE TO GO FROM HERE

Once you have a firm grasp on the basic rules, it's time to tackle the advanced rules. You knew it wasn't going to be that easy. Again, these rules are pretty straightforward, but they're unlike rules in games that most parents understand, so it may take you some time to master them.

We discuss these rules in the "Becoming a **Pokémon** Master" chapter. The CD and the videotape can also help you learn these rules. There are two items covered in the advanced rules: special attacks (those that do more than just damage a defending Pokémon) and Resistance and Weakness.

The special attacks are sleep, paralyze, confuse, and poison. We won't go into details here, but in essence, sleep and paralyze make a Pokémon unable to attack (it's asleep or can't move) for a brief period of time. Confuse makes your Pokémon unsure about how to attack (and it can damage itself instead). Poison just does more damage, but once a Pokémon gets poisoned, it keeps taking damage from the poison until you cure it.

TIP
You can find a free demo to get you started at the **Pokémon** TCG website, www.wizards.com/ Pokemon.

27

Resistance and Weakness make Pokémon tougher against some types of Pokémon and weaker against others. It's very simple. If a Pokémon has a Weakness against another Pokémon, it takes double damage from that Pokémon. If a Pokémon has a Resistance to another Pokémon, all damage from that Pokémon is reduced by 30 points.

The only tricky part about Weakness and Resistance is figuring out the symbols on the cards. These refer to the various types of Pokémon:

These symbols and colors match the symbols and colors on the Energy cards so you can easily figure out what kind of Energy a Pokémon needs by looking at the symbols.

Energy Type	Color	Symbol
Fighting	Orange	✊
Fire	Red	🔥
Grass	Green	🍃
Lightning	Yellow	⚡
Psychic	Purple	👁
Water	Blue	💧
Colorless	Gray	✳

Plus, the Weaknesses and Resistances follow a fairly obvious pattern much like rock-paper-scissors.

- **Water** Pokémon are generally good against Fire Pokémon (water puts out fire).
- **Fire** Pokémon are generally good against Grass Pokémon (fire burns up grass).
- **Grass** Pokémon are generally good against

Fighting Pokémon (grass is hard to trample).

- **Fighting** Pokémon are generally good against Lightning Pokémon (they're grounded).
- **Lightning** Pokémon are generally good against Water Pokémon (water conducts electricity).

To really understand all these Resistances and Weaknesses, we strongly suggest you watch the **Pokémon** animated series. The Pokémon in the trading card game follow closely the strengths and weaknesses of their counterparts on the show.

NOW YOU NEED A DECK

Now you know a little more about the basic concepts of the **Pokémon** trading card game. If you read through the first couple of chapters in the second section of this book, you'll be on your way to mastering the game. If you still have trouble, try one of the demos or watch the instructional videotape.

But then what? To play **Pokémon** you need a deck. You can take the two 30-card decks in the Starter game and combine them into a regulation 60 card deck. This is actually a good way to get your first 60-card deck. But eventually you may get tired of that deck (or getting beaten by your 8-year-old daughter). What do you do next?

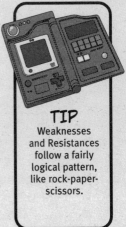

TIP
Weaknesses and Resistances follow a fairly logical pattern, like rock-paper-scissors.

Try the theme decks that you can buy in the store. These decks are ready to play. They still may not be as strong as the decks some 12-year-olds have built, but you can have a lot of fun with them. Once you understand the game well enough, you can tear a theme deck apart to see how it was put together.

If you're ready to build your own deck, take a look at the "Building Your Own Deck" chapter for some tips on how to get started. You might also want to read some Pokémon strategy articles in magazines such as *TopDeck* so you can become a true Pokémon Master (or at least beat your son or daughter once in a while).

GROUND RULES
FOR TRADING

• • • • • • • • • • • • • • •

So now you know how to play the **Pokémon** TCG (or at least you're on your way). Maybe you've even helped your child build or fine tune a deck (we call it "tuning the deck"). But playing the game and building decks are only half the fun of a trading card game. The other part is right there in the name. **Pokémon** is a game played with cards that you can trade.

Of course that means you have to learn some more rules—the ground rules of trading. Unfortunately, there aren't any hard and fast rules for trading, so there's nothing in any of the rulebooks. In this chapter, we'll give you the trading vocabulary you'll need and teach you what every Pokémon fan already knows about trading. We'll also give you some hints about how to get the most out of your Pokémon dollar. Plus, we've produced a list of rules to help keep your kids and their cards safe.

VOCABULARY

To understand how **Pokémon** TCG card trading works, you first need to learn some terms and concepts about the cards and how they are distributed. **Pokémon** TCG cards have different values based on a variety of conditions.

Rarity. **Pokémon** TCG cards are printed in four rarities: common, uncommon, rare, and ultra-rare (holofoil) cards. Rare cards are much harder to find when opening booster packs than common and uncommon cards because of the distribution of these cards in the packs (1 rare, 3 uncommon, and 7 common cards to a booster). So these cards are tougher to get in a trade and more expensive to purchase on the secondary single card market. In general, an average rare card will be worth about $3 to $5.

Holofoil. Your kids may call these "shinies" because they sparkle in the light. These are the most sought-after (and most expensive) **Pokémon** TCG cards because they are rarer than rare cards (and because they look so cool). Only about 1 in 3 booster packs will have a holofoil card (in place of the

Rarity Symbol

The Rarity symbol makes it easy to tell if you have a fair trade.

The different symbols are ● Common, ◆ Uncommon, and ★ Rare.

Fair Trades

3 ● Commons = 1 ◆ Uncommon

3 ◆ Uncommons = 1 ★ Rare

3 ★ Rares = 1 Holofoil (shiny)

Commons = Uncommon

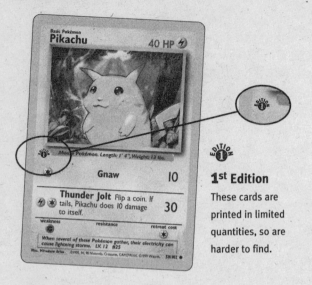

1st Edition

These cards are printed in limited quantities, so are harder to find.

regular rare card in that pack), so they're worth more to buy or trade. In expansion sets like *Jungle* or *Fossil*, each rare card has both a normal and holofoil version. Base Set holofoil cards have no nonholofoil version in that set. Holofoil cards are worth about $10 to $15, but some Base Set holofoils, like Charizard, can go for $50 or more.

1st Edition. The last wrinkle in the rarity of cards is the 1st Edition cards. Whenever a new set of **Pokémon** TCG cards is printed, a small set of cards are printed with the 1st Edition logo on them. This smaller print run is intended solely for collectors who crave the added value (and challenge) associated with collecting a set of 1st Edition cards.

Unlimited cards, which are printed in much larger quantities (and sometimes reprinted to meet extra demand) are the same exact cards, just without the 1st Edition logo. Since there are fewer 1st Edition cards in circulation, they are worth more than their unlimited counterparts.

Booster. Booster packs have a random assortment of 11 cards. However, a booster pack only has 1 rare card, which is why rares tend to be more valuable (and harder to collect). The other 10 cards in a booster are 3 uncommon and 7 common cards. Booster packs are the best way to begin building a collection because the cards are randomly inserted into the packs (within the rarity structure) so each booster will give you new cards to add to your collection...up to a point. Once you start getting too many repeats, you need to switch over to trading to finish your collection.

Theme Deck. Unlike booster packs, each particular theme deck (like "Zap!" or "Water Blast") contains the same 60 cards They are not a random assortment so buying multiple decks with the same name just gives you multiple copies of the same cards. The theme decks are about the best way to start playing the **Pokémon**

TIP
The best way to begin building a collection is with booster packs. Every pack will give you new cards to add to your collection or to trade for cards you need.

POKÉMON
TRADING CARD GAME

BASIC SET UNLIMITED

Item	High	Med	Low	TR	+/-
Booster Pack	$4.00	$3.50	$2.99	3	
Starter Deck	11.00	9.99	8.99	0	
Blackout PCD	12.00	9.99	9.99	3	
Brushfire PCD	12.00	9.99	9.99	3	
Overgrowth PCD	12.00	9.99	9.99	3	
Zap! PCD	12.99	9.99	9.99	0	

(Price list continues with individual card listings for Basic Set, Jungle, and other sets — columns: High, Med, Low, TR, +/-)

JUNGLE UNLIMITED

Item	High	Med	Low	TR	+/-
Complete Set	$185	$150	$100	5	
Booster Display	113	105	100	5	
Booster Pack	3.09	3.29	2.99	4	0.29
Power Reserve PCD	12.99	10.00	9.99	3	
Water Blast PCD	12.00	9.99	9.99	3	

Monetary Value

Price Guides, like this one from *TopDeck* magazine, can be very useful for estimating the relative value of cards for a trade.

TCG quickly because they're fun to play and let you get started playing without building decks. The theme decks each have one holofoil card inside, so they're also a good way to get multiple copies of those cards. However, since those holofoils are easier to get, they generally will be worth less on the secondary market.

TIP
Before you ever buy a card with cash, check a price guide.

Singles. Some card stores and Internet sites sell "singles" (individual cards from a booster pack) to collectors. These stores will buy cards from players and collectors and will also open up packs to sell the cards one at a time. This is a tough business because the prices of singles vary a lot from region to region, and usually only the rare and holofoil cards are worth selling since most people have plenty of common and uncommon cards. Buying singles is one way to get a specific card you need for your collection. But be sure you check a price guide so you know the going price for a card before you buy.

Secondary Market. All of the card stores, Internet sites, and individuals that buy, sell, or trade cards make up the secondary market. Prices for cards on the secondary market vary from region to region and even from store to store. The price of a given card depends on its rarity, its popularity among players and collectors, its abilities in the game, and its condition. Trying to get a handle on the value of cards in the secondary market is what trading is all about.

Condition. Most TCG card collectors want "mint condition" cards, which are cards just out of a booster pack (rarely if ever touched by human hands). We discuss condition in more depth in the "Catching 'Em All" chapter, but basically there are four levels: mint, near mint, excellent, and fine. Most kids and players don't worry about condition, so a fine card (with a few scuff marks on the card back) will be as good as a mint card. You can often get good trades from a pure collector by trading mint cards straight from a pack for his or her fine condition cards.

Price Guide. Price guides list prices for single cards. They are based on data from a limited number of stores (usually spanning the country), so they are not infallible. But, by comparing the median price of all the cards in a trade, you can use a price guide like the one in *TopDeck* magazine to make sure you or your kids don't get ripped off when trading or buying singles on the secondary market. Remember, these are the prices that stores will sell the cards for, not what they would pay to purchase those same cards.

BUY OR TRADE - WHAT SHOULD YOU DO?

Now that you better understand how TCG cards turn into valuable collector's items, you need to ask yourself how far you want to go into collecting (or how far you want to let your kids go). If collecting really excites you, you may want to try to collect a complete set of cards from an expansion like *Fossil*. If the bug hits hard, you might even want to collect a complete *Fossil* 1st Edition set.

However, you don't have to go that far to enjoy collecting **Pokémon** TCG cards. You can set challenges for yourself or your kids at just about any level. For example, you can just collect all the Water Pokémon or all the Fighting Pokémon in a set. For players, it's almost always more important to find a certain card from a set that fits into their favorite deck than to try to "catch 'em all."

Where you end up on this spectrum of collectors will determine whether you buy more booster packs or single cards and how you trade with other collectors. If you want to collect a complete set of cards, you're almost always better off buying booster packs at first (to get a good base of cards) and then trading or buying single cards to complete your set.

A good rule of thumb is to find out how many rare cards are in a set (a good check list like the one in this book or those printed in *TopDeck* magazine will list card rar-

TIP
Price guides are not infallible but they will give you a very strong idea of the median price for any specific card.

ities) and buy that many booster packs to start. For example, the *Fossil* set has 15 rare cards, so buy 15 packs. This will give you 15 rare cards to start your collection and use for trades. Plus, you should have multiple copies of every uncommon and common card in the set.

WHAT MAKES A FAIR TRADE?

Once you are ready to start trading, you really just need one piece of advice: Know how much the cards are worth. Of course, as we said earlier, determining the value of a card can be a tricky proposition. So let's talk a little more about what makes a good trade and how to tell how much a card is worth

When it comes to trading card games, there are a lot more factors involved in fair trading than just the value of the cards. For example, a Pokémon's popularity can impact the value of the card for some kids. If a child really likes Cubone, he or she may be willing to trade a more valuable card to get Cubone. This is just fine as long as everyone is happy afterwards (including you!).

Other things that impact the fairness of a trade include the rarity of the cards involved, whether the card is a holofoil or 1st Edition card, and how powerful the card is when playing the game. You should generally try to trade rare for rare, holofoil for holofoil, and so on. But the popularity of the card or its power in the game may break these rules. For example, the Trainer card Bill is a very useful card in the game because it gives you more choices during your turn. So, it is more valuable than the average common card.

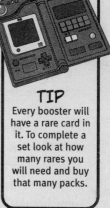

TIP
Every booster will have a rare card in it. To complete a set look at how many rares you will need and buy that many packs.

Be aware, some kids are more savvy about all these nuances than others, and there are kids out there who may try to take advantage of younger or less experienced kids. So, make sure your children understand the monetary, emotional, and play value of the cards before you let them trade without supervision.

In the end, though, a fair trade is one that makes both people involved in the trade happy afterward. If you are a serious collector and are worried about the monetary value of your (or your child's) collection, you may feel you need to be happy about the outcome as well. If so, you might want to take a more active role in your child's trades.

POKÉMON TCG TRADING RULES

There are no hard and fast rules for **Pokémon** TCG card trading. The value of a card can change from store to store, region to region, and day to day. If you want to become a true collector, you'll need to stay up to date with all the trends, all the new sets, and who likes what kinds of cards in your area.

However, if you or your child just want to trade cards without getting burned, you should look at the guidelines below and read through the trading tips presented in the "Catching 'Em All" chapter.

Know your limits. The value of **Pokémon** TCG cards varies from a quarter up to hundreds of dollars (for Japanese holofoils mostly). As a parent, you need to know your limits so you can set limits for your children. If you trust your child to responsibly handle $50 cards, then you can set fairly broad limits. If you are worried when your child takes a $5 bill to school for a field trip, you might need to set stricter guidelines. The age of your child will greatly affect this decision.

Know your kid's friends. Parents seem busier these days, so it's hard to get to know all of your kid's friends. But it is important to know who these kids are and what kind of limits their parents have imposed to make sure that trades don't go horribly wrong. We don't advocate making kids go back on trades (and you shouldn't have to if you set your limits correctly), but it's best if you know you can trust the kids your child trades with.

Make sure your kids know how to determine rarity. To tell the rarity of a **Pokémon** card, look at the symbol in the lower right corner of the card. A circle (●) appears on common cards. A diamond

(♦) appears on uncommon cards. A star (★) appears on rare cards. Holofoils have the star (★) as well, but have that special shiny foil on the card image. If your child can't tell the difference between the rarities, he or she probably isn't ready to trade yet (at least not with rares or holofoils).

Trade rare for rare; holofoil for holofoil, uncommon for uncommon. A common is worth about 25 cents. An uncommon is worth about $1. A rare is worth about $5. The average holofoil is worth $10-$15. Trades don't have to be even in price, but would you give someone a five dollar bill for a quarter? Probably not. This is the most basic way to determine if a trade is fair or not. If your child always trades this way, he or she can't get burned too badly, especially if you're not worried about the ultimate value of the collection.

Parents must be present for any trade involving a holofoil. Some of these cards are listed in price guides for $50 to $80 (or more for 1st Edition holofoils). If you feel comfortable giving your child that much money to buy something, that's fine. If your comfort level is around $5 (about the value of most non-holo rares), then you can let your child trade rare cards unsupervised. If your comfort level is at

TIP
In general, a common card is worth about 25 cents, while a rare is worth about $5, so be sure you and your child know how to determine a card's rarity.

the $1 range, stick to uncommons and commons.

Never trade away the last card of its kind. If you are trying to complete a set, then your last copy of a card is the most valuable one (for you) that you have. It's almost always better to trade away extra copies of a card to get a card you don't have than to trade away the last copy of a card in your collection. So, if you only have one Charizard, it doesn't make sense to trade it away for anything except another card that you don't have. Even then, that's probably a bad trade.

If you're not sure about a trade, ask for help. This is where price guides come in handy. Price guides can give you a general idea of how fair a trade is by checking the value of all the cards involved in the trade. Most price guides give high, median, and low prices. Make sure to check the same column for each card. The *TopDeck* price guide also has tradability ratings, which are a measure of each card's usefulness in the game. If no price guide is available, ask someone who knows more about prices, like the owner of a card shop, for help.

Don't feel you *have* to trade if you don't want to. Older kids may try to pressure younger (or less experienced) kids into trades. Make sure your children know that if they feel uncomfortable or unhappy about a trade, *they can just say "No!"*

TRUST YOUR CHILDREN

One final note about trading. We have heard people say that when kids get together to trade, they don't whine, pout, or throw tantrums. It takes a certain level of sophistication to trade well and most kids realize they need to approach this activity as adults if they want to succeed.

TIP
Never trade your last card of its kind if you're trying to complete a set. Try to trade multiple cards of a less-rare variety first.

While it is a good idea to set certain limits on your children's trades based on your financial comfort level, you should avoid the temptation to second guess completed trades. If you and another parent ask two kids to give back a bad trade, you invalidate the decisions those two kids made. Certainly you should set limits. And you should help your children learn from their mistakes. But if you interfere too much, you might hold your child back in what can be one of life's great learning experiences.

4

LEARNING WITH POKÉMON

WHILE **POKÉMON** MAY BE A LOT OF FUN with all the cool creatures to collect, all the games to play, and all the animated episodes to watch, we just wouldn't be parents if we didn't find some way to turn all this fun into an educational experience.

In this chapter, we'll present an assortment of activities you can try with your kids that can help you and your children learn with **Pokémon**. Of course, these aren't the only activities you can try, and some of these might not work for you. But we hope you'll find some activities that you like and that others will spark your imagination about the possibilities of using **Pokémon** to teach.

PLAY THE GAME

The **Pokémon** TCG could be the Go Fish or Old

Maid of the new millennium. As we've said already, the **Pokémon** TCG is similar to other games designed for young players because it helps children learn the importance of rules *and* gives them an incentive to improve their reading and math skills.

All you need to do to help guide your child's development is learn the rules and build two decks that are evenly matched against each other. The pre-built theme decks are designed that way. As you play, you can help your child read the cards and do the math needed during Pokémon battles. You can also teach your child lessons about playing by the rules, and about winning and losing.

To keep your children interested in the game, you may want to let them win. But learning how to lose a game is just as important in a child's development as learning how to win games (and how to behave when you do win). How you teach those social skills to your children is your business. You can try to emphasize the joy of competing and the fun you have playing together to make sure they understand that there is more to playing a game than just winning.

TIP

Teaching your child how to win is important, but don't neglect the importance of losing with patience. The game should always remain fun.

Damage Counters

Using change can visually teach children how to count money.

MONEY FOR DAMAGE

Another way you can use the **Pokémon** TCG to teach your children valuable lessons about life is to use dimes for damage counters. The interesting thing about Pokémon battles is that all Pokémon damage is counted in increments of 10. If your child is just learning about the value of money, this can help reinforce the lessons.

Instead of damage counters, get out a bag of change. When a Pokémon damages another Pokémon, have your child count out the damage in dimes. Once you hit 50 damage, ask your child to substitute two quarters for the five dimes. Ask your child what those coins are. Ask him or her what half of 50 is. Show your child that 25 cents equals one quarter. You can even substitute 2 nickels for 1 dime to show that relationship.

If you have really large Pokémon battling, you may even be able to get a dollar bill out and explore its relationship to the quarters and dimes.

TIP
Building decks is an exercise that combines creativity with basic math skills.

BUILD A DECK

Once you understand how **Pokémon** decks are built, you can start building decks with your children. Not only is this quality time you can spend with your kids, but deck building takes creativity and some math skills to do right.

Every **Pokémon** deck must have exactly 60 cards and needs a certain number of Basic, Stage 1, and Stage 2 Pokémon, Energy cards, and Trainer cards. So your child will need to use basic and advanced math skills (everything from addition and subtraction to fractions) while building a deck.

For a fun deck, ask your child to come up with a theme for the deck, like a deck based on the Pokémon that Brock uses in the animated series. Pick out about 20 Basic Pokémon cards that follow the theme and about four to six Stage 1 and Stage 2 Pokémon. Ask you child to add these up to see how many cards the deck has so far.

Pokémon Puzzles

Puzzles, like this one from *TopDeck* magazine, are just learning
exercises disguised as a fun activity.

You also need 24 to 28 Energy cards, which need to match the type of Basic Pokémon in the deck (this is where the fractions come in). If half of the Pokémon are Fighting type and the other half are Fire type, your child will need to know that 12 is half of 24. The last few cards in the deck will be Trainers. If the deck has 52 cards at this point, ask your child how many Trainer cards he can add.

PUZZLES AND POKÉMON STORIES

Pokémon is more than just the trading card game cards. There are lots of activities and products with Pokémon themes in stores. You can use your child's love of Pokémon to nurture his or her interest in reading and puzzle solving.

Many magazines that discuss **Pokémon**, including *TopDeck* magazine, provide puzzles for younger readers. However, if a puzzle is too hard, the lack of control your child feels can frustrate him or her. We recommend you solve the puzzles first (it's okay to look at the answers) so you can help your child master them. But resist the temptation to help too much. Puzzles are great ways to teach children how to think logically and solve problems step by step. Plus

TIP
If you solve the puzzles first, you will increase your familiarity with the game, but also become more capable of helping out if your child needs it.

solving a puzzle can give a kid a huge ego boost, which helps build self-esteem.

Scholastic is publishing **Pokémon** stories, and what better way to use the Pokémon phenomenon than to get your kids to read a book? We think that reading is probably the most important skill a child can learn, and studies have shown that reading to your kids promotes in them a desire to learn to read. Since kids love the story of Ash Ketchum and his quest to become the greatest Pokémon Master, why not get your kids to transfer that interest from the television to a book?

MAKE YOUR CHILD THE HERO

Another way you can use stories to spend some fun time with your kids is to make them the heroes of their own Pokémon adventure. This can be a lot of fun as an ongoing nightly story before bedtime. You'll be amazed at how much your child will remember about the story so far. Everything from Pokémon caught to Gym Masters defeated will all be catalogued in your child's memory. In fact, this is a great game to play to help improve your child's memory.

If you need help telling the stories, you might want to check out a new game called the **Pokémon Jr. Adventure Game**, which is designed for children from 6 to 8 years old. This game provides adventures that are written like little short stories with your child as the main character. It even comes with Pokémon on special cards that you and your child can use in battles during the stories. Your kid gets to keep the Pokémon he or she captures as the stories progress, giving him or her a sense of accomplishment.

TIP

If your kid is a Pokémaniac, you can offer books and other reading material about Pokémon to transfer interest away from the television.

POKÉMON CARD TRIVIA

If *you* know the trivia surrounding Pokémon (or can get some of the cards to look at) you can take your kids on a trivia hunt. Watch the show and see how many different Pokémon each of you can spot. On car trips, you can pick a card, read through all the statistics (Hit Points, length and weight, attacks, Evolution Stages, and so on) and then ask a question like: "What is the Stage 1 Mushroom Pokémon with 60 hit Points?" Answer: Parasect.

You can also play 20 Questions and let your kids ask you yes or no questions about the Pokémon card you have in your hand ("Is it a Grass Pokémon?" "Is it a Basic Pokémon?") All the information is on the cards, so you should be able to answer every question your kids can ask (unless they throw plot points from the animated series at you).

GOING IT ON YOUR OWN

Well, we hope these activities have at least sparked your imagination about the possibilities of **Pokémon**. If you still need help learning to play **Pokémon**, take a look at the "Learn to Play Like a Master" section. This section is geared more toward teaching your children how to play and helping them improve their playing and deck building skills, but it is a good resource for anyone who wants to learn the game.

Then, in section three, we take you out into the world of Pokémon. In this section you will find information about the League, more tips on how to collect and trade **Pokémon** TCG cards (and a card check list), plus answers to some of the most frequently asked questions we hear.

Good luck.

SECTION TWO

· · · · · · · · · · · · · · · · · ·

LEARN TO PLAY LIKE A MASTER

LET S PLAY POKÉMON!

WELCOME, POKÉMON TRAINERS. That's right, when you play the **Pokémon** Trading Card Game (TCG) *you* are a Pokémon trainer! You've probably already started your work as a Pokémon trainer by collecting, saving, and trading **Pokémon** cards with your friends. Because, as every trainer knows, you've gotta catch 'em all!

But, once you've caught them, what do you do with them?

Well, if you want to become a real **Pokémon** TCG Master, you have to let your Pokémon fight against another trainer's Pokémon. In other words, you have to play the game. In this section we will discuss the basic and advanced rules of the game and give you some tips for building great decks and playing like a Pokémon Master.

WHAT IS A TRADING CARD GAME ?

You've played lots of card games before, so what makes the **Pokémon** TCG different?

The biggest change is that you don't play with just one deck of cards. Each player has a deck of his or her own! Your friends may have different cards in their decks when you play against them. Even if they have different cards, it's still the same game!

You probably already have a deck of your own. You may even have two or more decks that you bought in the store. You can play the **Pokémon** TCG with any of these decks. But you can use only one deck at a time.

START WITH A STARTER DECK

If you've never played the **Pokémon** TCG before, it really is best to begin with a Starter Deck. It uses the same cards as other **Pokémon** decks, and it makes learning to play much easier. Once you've played with the Starter Deck a few times, you will know the game much better. You'll be ready to try one of the other decks you see in the stores.

TIP
The Starter Deck gives you two 30-card decks, so you can learn how to play right away with a friend.

Maybe the coolest thing about a trading card game is that you can change the cards in your deck! That's one of the reasons you collect the cards. You can fill your deck with your favorite Pokémon and make it different from anyone else's deck in the whole world.

We'll talk more about building your own deck later in the book. First, let's talk about playing the game. If you already know how to play the **Pokémon** TCG, you might want to skip this chapter. But if you have questions about the rules or want some extra tips about how to play, read on!

SETTING UP

Before you play, be sure that you have enough space for the game. The **Pokémon** TCG doesn't take up a very large area, but you do need a flat open space big enough for both your cards *and* your opponent's cards.

Setting up is easiest if you have a **Pokémon** TCG playmat, which comes in the Starter Deck. It shows you exactly where all your cards need to go. Once you know how to play you might not need the playmat anymore, but it can still be helpful.

Lay all your game pieces in front of you, and have your friend do the same thing. You should both have your deck, some damage counters, and a coin or two. It's best to be sure that you have everything before you start playing so you don't have to stop the game in the middle while you look for a missing piece.

SHUFFLE

Before you start, both players should shuffle their decks. If you don't know how to shuffle, deal your cards one by one into four piles in front of you. When you're done, pick the piles up and do the same thing again. If you do this four or five times, you should have a well-shuffled deck.

TIP
Shuffle your deck well before you start to make sure you get a good selection of cards.

Once both players' decks are shuffled, you're ready to play.

DRAW

Both players draw 7 cards from their decks. Look at your cards. You should have a few different types of cards in your hand. There are three types of cards in the **Pokémon** TCG: Energy cards, Trainer cards, and Pokémon. If you only got one type of card in your draw, you probably haven't shuffled your deck well enough.

As long as you have one Basic Pokémon in your hand, you can continue with the game. (We'll talk about what a Basic Pokémon is in the next section.) If you do not have any Basic Pokémon in your hand, put your cards back in the deck. Pick the deck up and shuffle it again. When you're done, draw another 7 cards. If you still don't have a Basic Pokémon, reshuffle the deck again. Do this until you get a Basic Pokémon in your 7-card draw.

Every time you have to reshuffle, the other player can draw an extra 1 or 2 cards if he or she likes. Having a few extra cards gives your opponent a big lead over you. He or she will have more choices in the early part of the game. This is one reason why it is very important to shuffle your deck well.

CHOOSE A POKÉMON

Choose one of the Basic Pokémon in your hand. This will be the first Pokémon you send out to fight, so choose carefully.

Once you've made your choice, lay that card face down on the table. The game is about to start. During play you should follow the instructions that came with your **Pokémon** deck. It is much easier to read than this book when you are in the middle of a game. If you have any questions about what the instructions say, you can always come back to the book for help.

TYPES OF POKÉMON

This game is all about Pokémon. You want your Pokémon to battle and Knock Out your opponent's Pokémon. So, before we get into the game, let's talk a little about different types of Pokémon in the game. You must know the difference between them if you plan to become a **Pokémon** TCG Master.

BASIC POKÉMON

Like people, Pokémon start small and grow bigger as they get older. If you look at the upper left corner of your **Pokémon** cards you will see some small writing above the name of the Pokémon. If it says "Basic Pokémon" here, then this is the way the Pokémon looks when you first get it.

At the start of the game you can only play Basic Pokémon from your hand. In fact, every Pokémon in the game must start as a Basic Pokémon before it can grow bigger (or Evolve). It is very important that you have plenty of Basic Pokémon in your deck. Most decks use at least 16 Basic Pokémon. All of the decks you can buy in the stores come with more than enough Basic Pokémon.

Some Basic Pokémon are Bulbasaur, Charmander, Squirtle, Pikachu, and Hitmonchan.

STAGE 1 POKÉMON

When a Pokémon grows, it changes (like a kid turns into a teenager). It's still the same creature, but you can also tell it's a little different than it used to be.

TIP
All Pokémon start out as Basic Pokémon, so you need a lot of these in your deck. Use at least 16.

When Basic Pokémon Evolve, they become Stage 1 Pokémon.

In the game you can only use Stage 1 Pokémon only by playing them onto Basic Pokémon. This is called Evolving your Pokémon. In other words, you can't just send a Stage 1 Pokémon into play. You have to add it to a Pokémon that is already in play.

You Evolve a Basic Pokémon by placing the Stage 1 Pokémon on top of the Basic Pokémon it Evolves from. You can tell which Basic Pokémon a Stage 1 Pokémon Evolves from by reading the text above the name of the Pokémon or by looking at the picture beneath the words "Stage 1" next to its name on the card.

Some Stage 1 Pokémon are Ivysaur, Charmeleon, Wartortle, and Raichu. There is no Stage 1 Pokémon for Hitmonchan.

Basic Pokémon

These have no symbol. They just say "Basic Pokémon."

Evolution Symbol

This tells what type of Pokémon it is and show a picture of the Pokémon it Evolved from.

Evolved Pokémon

Charmeleon, the Stage 1 Evolution of Charmander, is more powerful and has more Hit Points.

STAGE 2 POKÉMON

As a Pokémon continues to grow it may change even more, the way a teenager turns into a grown-up. Some Stage 1 Pokémon can Evolve into Stage 2 Pokémon.

In the game you can use Stage 2 Pokémon only by playing them onto Stage 1 Pokémon. In other words, you can't just send a Stage 2 Pokémon into play. You have to add it to a Pokémon already in play. You Evolve Stage 1 Pokémon the same way you Evolve a Basic Pokémon—by placing the Stage 2 Pokémon on top of the Stage 1 Pokémon it Evolves from.

Some Stage 2 Pokémon are Venusaur, Charizard, and Blastoise. There is no Stage 2 Pokémon for Raichu.

Hit Points

As Pokémon Evolve they get bigger. Notice the difference in Hit Points.

Evolved Pokémon

Charizard is even more powerful than Charmeleon. Notice that Charizard's attack is much more expensive than Charmeleon's attack shown on the previous page.

YOUR FIRST POKÉMON

Okay, back to your first game. When both players have chosen their first Basic Pokémon, flip them both over. These are the Active Pokémon.

THE ACTIVE POKÉMON

This is the Pokémon that is ready to fight right now. When it's your turn to attack, your Active Pokémon may attack. When your opponent's Pokémon attacks, your Active Pokémon is the one that takes the damage. You should always know which of your Pokémon is Active, how many Hit Points it has (this is the red number on the upper right of the card—50HP means the Pokémon has 50 Hit Points), and how much damage it has taken.

POKÉMON ON THE BENCH

Any Pokémon you play from your hand to the table, other than the Active Pokémon, are said to be on the Bench. You can never have more than 5 Pokémon on the Bench at one time.

You can have more than one of the same type of Pokémon in play at the same time. In other words, you can have a Charmander as your Active Pokémon and also have a Charmander on the Bench. In fact, you can fill your whole Bench with Charmanders if you like. (This is not a very good idea, and we'll explain why in a little while. But it is okay to do this according to the rules.)

YOUR GOAL

In order to win the game you must Knock Out a certain number of your opponent's Pokémon. In the Starter Deck this number is 3, but in most **Pokémon** TCG games you must Knock Out 6 of your opponent's Pokémon to win.

TIP
Keep track of how many Hit Points your Active Pokémon has left. If it gets knocked out, your opponent gets a Prize.

Once you know how many Pokémon you must Knock Out, you should set aside that many cards from your deck as Prizes. Every time you Knock Out an opposing Pokémon, you take one prize. This gives you a bonus for getting one step closer to your goal, and it also helps you keep track of how you are doing. When all your prizes are gone, you have reached your goal.

Who goes first is just a matter of luck. Flip a coin and the winner goes first.

ON YOUR TURN

Your turn has 4 steps. Some of them are simple. Others will have you make some tough choices. But in the end, your turn is no more difficult than this:

1. Draw a Card
2. Play Cards
3. Attack
4. End Your Turn

DRAW A CARD

Always remember to draw a card. In the **Pokémon** trading card game, the cards in your hand tell you what choices you have. If you forget to draw a card, you lose out on at least one choice.

PLAY CARDS

You can do any of the following things in any order during your turn. (Some of the choices below are used only in advanced games, and we will talk about them in detail in the next chapter.)

- Put Basic Pokémon on the Bench (as many as you want; although you may have only five Pokémon on your Bench at a time).
- Evolve Pokémon (as many as you want; although you may not Evolve a Pokémon the same turn you play it or twice in one turn).
- Attach 1 Energy to one of your Pokémon (only once per turn).
- Play Trainer cards (as many as you want).
- Retreat your Active Pokémon (as many times as you want; although you have to pay the Retreat Cost every time you retreat a Pokémon).
- Use Pokémon Powers (as many as you want; although some Pokémon Powers may be used once only per turn).

ATTACK

We'll talk about how to attack in a little while.

END YOUR TURN

This isn't really something to do. It's just a reminder that your turn ends right after you attack. So, if you want to do something on your turn (like play another Trainer card), you must do it before you attack. You cannot do anything after you attack except end your turn.

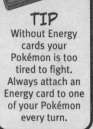

TIP
Without Energy cards your Pokémon is too tired to fight. Always attach an Energy card to one of your Pokémon every turn.

ENERGY FOR YOUR POKÉMON

Throughout the game you send your Pokémon out to battle. In order to use one of its attacks, your Pokémon needs Energy. Without Energy, your Pokémon is just too tired to fight. In the game we use Energy Cards to show how much Energy a Pokémon has. The cards also tell you what kind of Energy your Pokémon has.

TYPES OF ENERGY

There are seven different types of Energy, and each type has its own color and special symbol.

Energy Type	Color	Symbol
Fighting	Orange	🔨
Fire	Red	🔥
Grass	Green	🍃
Lightning	Yellow	⚡
Psychic	Purple	👁
Water	Blue	💧
Colorless	Gray	✴

PLAYING ENERGY CARDS

During your turn you can play one Energy Card from your hand and place it under one of your Pokémon. On the first turn this will probably be your Active Pokémon, but later in the game you will have to choose whether to give Energy to your Active Pokémon or one on the Bench. This decision will sometimes win or lose the game for you, so we'll talk more about it in a later chapter.

You can put as many different types of Energy as you like into your deck, but very often your Pokémon will need a certain type of Energy so it can use its attacks. It's important that your deck have the right kind of Energy for the Pokémon you are using. If it doesn't, your Pokémon may not be able to attack. We'll talk about how Pokémon use Energy in the next section.

Energized Pokémon

To attach an Energy card, simply place the card under the Pokémon. Pikachu can now Gnaw. (Any kind of Energy can be used as Colorless Energy.)

ATTACK!

Battling is what Pokémon do best. Each Pokémon has one or two attacks it can use in battle, and it's up to you to decide which one it will use each turn. Playing the game will be much easier if you know how all of your Pokémon's attacks work. Be sure to read the cards carefully before you decide which attack to use.

Once you decide, tell your opponent which attack you're using. But you'd better be sure your Pokémon has enough Energy to use that attack!

USING ENERGY

We already talked about how you give Energy to a Pokémon. Now let's talk about how your Pokémon uses that Energy.

Each Pokémon attack has a series of symbols next to it. These symbols tell you how much Energy (and what type of Energy) the Pokémon needs to use that attack.

Look at your Active Pokémon's attack. How many symbols are next to the attack name? Well, that's the number of Energy cards your Pokémon needs attached to it to use that attack. What kind of symbols are they? That's the kind of Energy your Pokémon needs attached. If

TIP
Remember to attach Energy to Pokémon on the Bench. You never know when you might need them to attack.

you ever see the symbol with the star ✪, that means you can use any kind of Energy for each of those symbols. If your Pokémon does not have the right number or kind of Energy, it cannot use that attack.

So if a Pokémon has ⬤✪ next to its attack, it needs 1 Water Energy and 1 other Energy of any kind in order to use that attack.

After the attack, your Pokémon and all the Energy attached to it stay in the Active Pokémon position. You discard Energy from a Pokémon only if:

- the text of the Pokémon Power or attack says to discard Energy to use that attack (for example, Charmeleon's Flame Thrower attack forces you to discard one Fire Energy to use it);

- you or your opponent plays a Trainer card that tells you to discard Energy (for example, Energy Removal); or

- you retreat your Active Pokémon and must pay a Retreat Cost.

WEAKNESS AND RESISTANCE

Some types of Pokémon are stronger against other types. To tell what type of Pokémon yours is, look at the upper right-hand corner of the card. Next to the Pokémon's Hit Points you will find a symbol that tells you what type of Pokémon you have.

After you tell your opponent what attack you're using, look at the bottom of his or her Pokémon card under the words "Weakness" and "Resistance." If

Weakness

Attacks from the type of Pokémon listed here double their attack damage. Clefairy would receive double damage from any attacks from Fighting Pokémon.

Resistance

You may subtract this number from damage this Pokémon receives if the attacking Pokémon is of this type. In this case, Clefairy reduces 30 points of damage from Psychic attacks.

you see the symbol that matches your Pokémon's type, then something special happens.

If the symbol appears under Weakness, then you double the damage your Pokémon does to your opponent's Active Pokémon this turn!

If the symbol appears under Resistance, then you subtract 30 points from the damage that your Pokémon does to your opponent's Active Pokémon this turn. If this takes your Pokémon's damage to zero or lower, then your Pokémon does no damage this turn.

As you play the game you'll learn which Pokémon have Weakness or Resistance to others. Knowing this will help you better decide which Pokémon to use in each battle.

RETREAT COSTS

You can retreat your Active Pokémon any time you want before you attack. It goes to your Bench and you must replace it with a Pokémon on your Bench. You can even Retreat more than once each turn, but most Pokémon have a Retreat Cost that must be paid each time.

You will find the words *Retreat Cost* in the bottom right-hand corner of the card. How many symbols are below these words? That's how many Energy cards attached to this Pokémon that you must discard to retreat that Pokémon. What kind of symbols are they? That is the type of Energy you must discard to retreat.

If that Pokémon does not have enough Energy to pay the retreat cost, then it must remain your Active Pokémon until you attach enough of the correct Energy cards to it or it gets Knocked Out. If there are no Energy symbols below the retreat cost, then the Pokémon can retreat for free.

DAMAGE

Each attack has a damage number listed toward the left of the card. For every 10 points of damage listed, place 1 damage counter on your opponent's Active Pokémon. In other words, if your attack does 30 damage, place 3 counters on your opponent's card.

Always remember to read the text printed next to the attack. It will tell you if there are other things you should do to go along with the damage you're Pokémon dishes out. We'll talk more about these special effects in the next chapter.

CHECK TOTAL DAMAGE

Count the number of damage counters on your opponent's Pokémon. Remember that each counter stands for 10 points of damage. If the total damage is equal to or higher than the Pokémon's Hit Points, you've Knocked Out the Pokémon! Your opponent must put that Pokémon along with all cards attached to it into his or her discard pile. He or she must then replace that Pokémon with one from his or her Bench.

PRIZES

Every time you Knock Out one of your opponent's Pokémon, you get to pick up one of the cards you set aside as Prizes. This helps you remember that you're one step closer to meeting your goal. It also gives you a reward by adding another card to your hand. Now you will have more choices next turn.

TIP
Sometimes you may have to attach Energy to a Pokémon just so you can discard that Energy to Retreat that Pokémon.

GET READY!

Unless you've reached your goal (Knock Out 3 or 6 of your opponent's

Pokémon), the game goes on. It is now your opponent's turn to play cards and attack your Pokémon.

While he or she thinks about just what to do, you can look at your cards and get ready for your next turn. Think about what cards you'll want to play and what moves you'll want to make.

EVOLUTION

Earlier we talked about different types of Pokémon and how Stage 1 and Stage 2 Pokémon can only come into the game through Evolution. But when can a Pokémon Evolve? And when is the best time to Evolve your Pokémon? And how do you decide which of your Pokémon to Evolve?

A Basic Pokémon cannot Evolve on the same turn that you put it into play from your hand. Any turn after that, you can play an Evolved Pokémon on that Pokémon. You also cannot Evolve a Pokémon twice in the same turn. So, if you Evolve Charmander into Charmeleon on one turn, you must wait until your next turn to Evolve Charmeleon into Charizard.

In general, you should Evolve your Active Pokémon only if it already has enough Energy attached to let the Evolved Pokémon attack right away. If the Pokémon is on the Bench, it is safer to Evolve it before it's full up on Energy since this makes it tougher. But remember that you still may have to send it into battle before you're ready to battle with it if your Active Pokémon gets Knocked Out.

If you're going to make the effort to Evolve a Benched Pokémon, be sure to also attach Energy to it about once every other turn. There's nothing sadder than losing a game because your Pokémon can't defend themselves.

TRAINING YOUR POKÉMON

So far we haven't talked about Trainer cards very much. One reason is that you can make a Pokémon deck without any Trainer cards at all and still play the game. So what good are Trainer cards? Plenty!

Trainer cards let you do all kinds of things to make your Pokémon stronger and tougher. They also let you do things to weaken your opponent or make better use of your deck. In other words, they let you bend the rules when you play them.

WINNING THE GAME

Earlier we talked about your goal in the game. If you can Knock Out a certain number of your opponent's Pokémon, then you win the game. While this is definitely your goal, it is not the only way to win the game. You also win if your opponent has no Pokémon in play or has no cards left to draw from the deck at the

TIP
Evolved Pokémon are bigger and tougher, but they also need more Energy to attack. Make sure you have enough Energy when you Evolve your Pokémon.

TIP
Keep your Bench loaded and your deck full of cards or you may lose a game by a technical Knock Out.

start of his or her turn.

Remember, these same rules apply to you. In other words, if you wind up with no Pokémon in play or no cards in your deck, then your opponent wins no matter how many of your Pokémon he or she has Knocked Out.

NO POKÉMON LEFT

If you Knock Out your opponent's Active Pokémon and he or she does not have any Pokémon on the Bench, then you win the game. This is most likely to happen early in the game if your opponent only drew 1 or 2 Basic Pokémon.

This rule shows why it is very important to have enough Basic Pokémon in your deck. It also teaches you that you should always have at least one Pokémon on your Bench at all times.

NO CARDS LEFT

The first step each turn is to draw a card. If your opponent starts a turn with no cards remaining in his or her deck, you win. This is only likely to happen in long games where the Pokémon are very evenly matched and both players have used Trainer cards to keep their Pokémon healthy.

You should be careful how many times you take advantage of rules that say you can choose to draw an extra card, or draw "up to" a certain number of cards. Every extra card you draw leaves you with one fewer card in your deck and gives your opponent an edge in a long game.

But extra cards help you win shorter games. We'll talk more about when to use cards like Bill and Professor Oak and when to hold off on using them in the "Play Like a Master" chapter.

BECOMING A
POKÉMON MASTER

OKAY. NOW YOU KNOW HOW TO PLAY the **Pokémon** trading card game. You started with the Starter Deck and worked your way up to one of the Theme Decks. You know how to attack, retreat, and Evolve your Pokémon, and you know how to win the game. But you're not a Pokémon Master yet.

There are still one or two advanced rules that we didn't talk about in the last chapter. A few Pokémon have Special Powers, for instance. And some attacks have effects that last for more than one turn.

Plus, it's not enough to know what your cards can do and how your deck plays. In order to become a true Pokémon Master, you need to know how your opponent's cards work. You need to be able to guess what he or she will do next, or what cards are in his or her hand. You can't do that unless you understand all the rules.

And that takes a lot of work.

Special Pokémon Power

If a Pokémon has a Special Power, it is listed above the attack. Venusaur's Pokémon Power: Energy Trans can move Grass Energy around, but only before you attack.

POKÉMON POWERS

Some Pokémon have a special Pokémon Power that they can use when they're in play. Remember, Benched Pokémon are in play, too, so they can use Pokémon Powers if they have any. You'll find the Pokémon Power just below the picture of your Pokémon and above that Pokémon's attacks. Usually, but not always, only Stage 2 Pokémon have Pokémon Powers.

Remember, a Pokémon Power isn't the same as an attack, so if you use a Pokémon Power, you can still attack! In fact, many of the Powers are meant to be used before you attack. Each Pokémon Power is different, though, so you should read carefully to see how each Power works.

Many Pokémon Powers can be used more than once per turn. The Pokémon Power text will always tell you if there is a limit to the number of times it can be used in one turn. If no limit is listed, then you can use the Power as many times as you like each turn.

SLEEP, CONFUSION, AND PARALYSIS

Some attacks cause the Defending Pokémon to become Asleep, Confused, or Paralyzed. These attacks can only strike the Active Pokémon, never those on the Bench. In fact, if an Active Pokémon that is Asleep, Confused, or Paralyzed goes to the Bench, these effects are removed from it.

Evolving a Pokémon also means that it's no longer Asleep, Confused, or Paralyzed.

Retreat Cost

When your Active Pokémon is Asleep or Paralyzed, it cannot retreat or attack. If it is Confused, it can only retreat or attack half the time, but you take a chance that it will hurt itself. When your Pokémon becomes Poisoned, it can retreat and attack, but it will continue to get hurt until it goes to your Bench or Evolves.

If a Pokémon is Asleep, Confused, or Paralyzed and a new attack is made against it that causes it to become Asleep, Confused, or Paralyzed, the old effect is erased and only the new one counts. These are the only attack effects that erase each other. For example, a Pokémon can be Confused and Poisoned at the same time.

TIP

You can keep your Pokémon with a Pokémon Power safe on the bench and use that power every turn. But beware of Gust of Wind!

ASLEEP

If a Pokémon is Asleep, it can't attack or retreat. As soon as a Pokémon is Asleep, turn it sideways to show that it's Asleep. After each player's turn, flip a coin. (This means after your opponent's turn *and* after your turn.) On heads, the Pokémon wakes up (turn the card back right-side up), but on tails it's still Asleep, and you'll have to wait until after the next turn to try to wake it up again.

CONFUSED

If a Pokémon is Confused, you have to flip a coin whenever you try to attack with it or whenever you try to make it retreat. Turn a Confused Pokémon with its head pointed toward you to show it's confused.

When you try to make a Confused Pokémon retreat, you first have to pay the Retreat Cost by discarding Energy cards. Then flip a coin. On heads, you may retreat the Pokémon as normal. On tails, the retreat fails and that Pokémon can't try to retreat again that turn.

When you attack with a Confused Pokémon, you also flip a coin. On heads, the attack works normally, but on tails your Pokémon attacks itself with an attack that does 20 damage. If your Pokémon has a Weakness or Resistance to its own type, or if there's some other effect that would alter the attack, apply these effects as usual. For example, many Psychic Pokémon have Weakness to Psychic attacks, so if Mr. Mime gets Confused and attacks itself, it will do 40 damage to itself.

PARALYZED

If a Pokémon is Paralyzed, it can't attack or retreat. Turn the Pokémon sideways (in the opposite direction from an Asleep Pokémon) to show that it's Paralyzed. If an Active Pokémon gets Paralyzed, it recovers after its player's next turn. When the Pokémon recovers, turn the card right-side up again. For example, if your opponent's Oddish Paralyzes your Pikachu, your Pikachu will stay Paralyzed until after your next turn.

POISON

Some attacks cause Pokémon to be Poisoned. These attacks can only strike the Active Pokémon, never

Poison Counters

Anything can be used to show that the Active Pokémon is Poisoned. Here we've used a different colored glass bead.

Damage Counters

These show that Pikachu has received 20 points of damage.

those on the Bench. If a Poisoned Active Pokémon goes to the Bench, it is no longer Poisoned. Evolving a Pokémon also means it's no longer Poisoned.

If a Pokémon gets Poisoned and a new attack is made against it that causes it to become Poisoned, the old Poison condition goes away and only the new one counts. In other words, a Pokémon can never be doubly Poisoned. Only another Poison attack can erase such a condition. It is fine for a Pokémon to be Poisoned and suffer from another special attack. For example, a Pokémon can be Poisoned and Paralyzed at the same time.

If a Pokémon is Poisoned, place a "poison marker" on it to show that it's Poisoned. As long as it is still Poisoned, the Pokémon takes 10 damage after each player's turn, ignoring Weakness and Resistance. For example, if your Pikachu gets Poisoned by your opponent's Beedrill, Pikachu will take 10 damage after your opponent's turn and 10 damage after your turn (unless you can remove the Poison effect before the end of your turn). So, you can see that Poisoned Pokémon can take a lot of damage very fast.

KNOW THE CARDS

Once you understand all the rules, you should begin to learn all the cards. Read them all several times until you understand what each card does and how to use it. You'll also find that when you know how your opponent's cards work, you can guess what he or she is about to do next and prepare yourself for it. Magazines like *TopDeck* magazine will print pictures of all the cards in a new set when that set comes out. Get a copy of one of these magazines so you can read all the cards.

PLAY COMBINATIONS

When you know the cards, you will see choices in every game you play. Each card will have more power than what is written on it, because you will be able to think about playing 2 and 3 cards together.

For example, you can play the Defender Trainer card (which reduces damage done by attacks by 20) on your Active Magnemite. When Magnemite uses its Self Destruct attack, it will do 40 damage to the defending Pokémon, 10 damage to all Benched Pokémon, and 40 damage to itself. Defender will reduce the damage Magnemite does to itself by 20

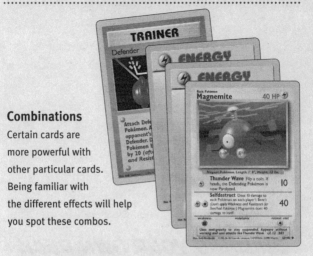

Combinations

Certain cards are more powerful with other particular cards. Being familiar with the different effects will help you spot these combos.

points, so Magnemite may not get Knocked Out.

This is called playing a combination. It is something that all Pokémon Masters do to plan an attack that can do more than one thing, like Knock Out the defending Pokémon and save their Active Pokémon.

To play combinations, though, you have to understand how all the cards in your deck work. You can even build combinations into your deck (and we'll talk more about this in the next chapter). Then, before the game starts you can have one or two special combinations figured out in your head that you will use if you get the right cards during the game.

BUILDING YOUR OWN DECK

By now, we hope you see that playing the **Pokémon** trading card game can be a lot of fun. But the best thing is that playing is only half the fun. Making a deck of your own is something that you can do during those times when there's no one else to play with. And some folks think that deck building is as much fun as playing the game—maybe even more!

GETTING STARTED

Your deck has to have *exactly* 60 cards, and you can't have more than 4 of any one card other than basic Energy cards in your deck. A card counts as the same as another card if it has the same name—

it doesn't matter whether the cards have different art or attacks, or even if they come from different sets.

For example, there are several different types of Pikachu cards. But whether you use Base Set Pikachu, *Jungle* Pikachu, or the Warner Brothers promotional Pikachu, they all count as Pikachu.

To make a new deck, first notice that all the cards other than the Trainer cards have Energy symbols shown on them. Your deck should probably include one or two of the basic Energy types, and you can choose to add some Colorless Pokémon if you like.

If you choose just one Energy type, you will always have the right kind of Energy for your Pokémon, but not as much variety. Plus, your deck might be weak against some decks because most of your Pokémon will have Weakness against the same type of Pokémon. If you have several Energy types, you'll have more Pokémon to choose from, but you'll run the risk of sometimes not drawing the right type of Energy for your Pokémon.

TIP
Using Pokémon of different Energy types gives you choices against more opponents. But don't use too many different Energy types.

Two Energy types (plus Colorless) are usually best because this limits the chance of having the wrong Energy cards in your hand, but gives you options against decks that might give one of your Energy types some problems. Also, be sure your deck has enough Energy cards (most decks need 25 to 30).

BE CREATIVE

Sometimes the hardest part of building a deck is getting started. You have the whole world of Pokémon to choose from, and you can pick only 60 cards to go into your deck! How do you start making those choices?

Sometimes just thinking of a name or a theme for your deck will be enough to give you ideas about what to put in it. For example, maybe you like Brock in the **Pokémon** animated series and want to make a deck with Pokémon he uses. You'll probably want to make a Fire and Fighting deck and start with Geodude and Vulpix.

PICKING YOUR POKÉMON

The best advice we can give is to start with one or two Pokémon you like. Pokémon have styles and personalities all their own, just like people. If you like a certain Pokémon, it will probably fit in very well with your style of play. You'll find that you enjoy both winning and losing more if you like working with the Pokémon in your deck.

When you build a **Pokémon** deck, you can't just throw any old group of cards together and call them winners. If nothing else, you have to make sure you restrict yourself to just one or two types of Pokémon (with maybe some Colorless ones thrown in) and use the right type of Energy. But it's also important that your cards cover for each other's Weaknesses as much as possible.

> **TIP**
> Make sure you check your Pokémon's Weaknesses and Resistances to make sure one type of Pokémon won't completely wreck your whole bench.

For example, let's say you want to build a deck that has several big Fire Pokémon. These Pokémon will be vulnerable against players who use lots of Water Pokémon, so it would be a good idea to use some Lightning Pokémon in your deck to handle the Water Pokémon decks. Adding one or two Colorless Pokémon can also protect you from other types of Pokémon your friends like to use.

AVOID AN ENERGY CRISIS

One of the biggest risks you can take when building a deck is to cut back too far on Energy. The reason to skimp on Energy is obvious: Fewer Energy cards mean more room for cool Pokémon and Trainers. But if you cut back too far, you won't draw enough Energy for those Pokémon to use their attacks, and if that happens, even those extra Trainer cards won't save you.

Generally, you want to have at least 25 Energy

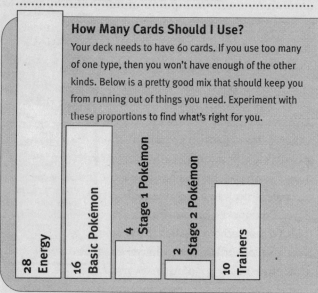

How Many Cards Should I Use?

Your deck needs to have 60 cards. If you use too many of one type, then you won't have enough of the other kinds. Below is a pretty good mix that should keep you from running out of things you need. Experiment with these proportions to find what's right for you.

28 Energy

16 Basic Pokémon

4 Stage 1 Pokémon

2 Stage 2 Pokémon

10 Trainers

cards (the decks you can buy come with 28). If you are using more than one type of Pokémon, you also need to use more than one type of Energy. A basic rule is to match the proportion of Pokémon and Energy cards. If half of your Pokémon are Fire type and half are Water type, then half of your Energy cards (about 12) should be Fire Energy and half (another 12) should be Water Energy.

BUILDING COMBOS

We talked a little bit in the last chapter about how you can use 2 or more cards together (combos) to make an effect that is really cool. Well, to do that, you need to build combos into your deck, and the best way to do that is to start with one central combo and build onto it. For example, look at the Magnemite and Defender combo we talked about in the last chapter. By using Defender, your Magnemite can survive its own Self Destruct attack (and maybe use it again on your next turn).

Once you have your central combo, think about other cards that will work well with those two cards. Magnemite damages your Benched Pokémon as well as your Opponent's Benched Pokémon. So if you have some Pokémon Centers in your deck, you might be able to remove all the damage on your Benched Pokémon (as well as Magnemite) next turn.

Since Magnemite damages your opponent's Benched Pokémon, you might want some control over which Pokémon your opponent has on the Bench. You can use Gust of Wind to move a Benched Pokémon (maybe one with only 40 HP left) into the Arena. If the Active Pokémon that you just Benched had only 10 HP left, you can now Knock Out 2 Pokémon with just one attack when Magnemite Self Destructs.

TIP
For a combo to work you need both cards in your hand at the same time, so put as many of each card as you can in the deck.

So, starting with just Magnemite and Defender, we now have 4 cards that can all work together to make some amazing things happen. By just starting with one simple combo, we have built a series of combos that all work well together.

WORK THE BENCH

It's easy to think of the Bench as a place where your Pokémon cool their heels until it's their turn to fight. But there's a lot more to Bench strategy than just replacing an Active Pokémon that's almost Knocked Out or Poisoned with a fresh one.

An interesting deck tactic is to include a few Pokémon that have lots of Hit Points. These Pokémon can hold the fort while you spend a few turns building up the Energy of the Pokémon on your Bench. Onix is especially good for this. With its 90 HP and its damage-preventing attack, it can last a long time against pretty much any Pokémon.

So now you know some more about how to make a **Pokémon** deck. In the next chapter we'll show you some tips for playing that deck.

PLAY LIKE A MASTER

OKAY, NOW YOU KNOW THE RULES, you know how to make your own deck, and you're ready to play. You'll win some and you'll lose some—that's just the way games go. Before you start, though, here are some tips that may help you win more **Pokémon** games than you lose.

ENERGY

If you did a good job of deck building, then you have the right amount of Energy and, maybe more importantly, the right types of Energy. In many games, whether you win or lose will depend on how well you use that Energy.

Except in very strange circumstances, you should play an Energy card every turn if you have one. Be sure, though, that you think about where you're placing that Energy. Powering up an Active

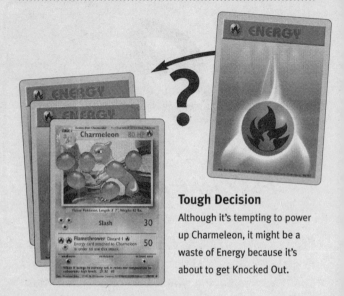

Tough Decision

Although it's tempting to power up Charmeleon, it might be a waste of Energy because it's about to get Knocked Out.

Pokémon that is likely to get Knocked Out next turn is a waste of time and Energy. Always try to have at least one Benched Pokémon with enough Energy attached that can attack at a moment's notice.

To get a good idea of what your opponent plans to do next, pay attention to where his or her Energy is going. If he or she spends 2 or 3 turns attaching Energy to the same Benched Pokémon, that's a big hint that your opponent will attack with that Pokémon or Evolve it very soon. Remember that your opponent will be watching what you do with your Energy, too.

TRAINER CARDS

The biggest strategy with Trainer cards is in deciding which ones to put in your deck. Once you begin play, you should be looking for the best time to play your cards. Remember, each time you play a Trainer card it's like bending the rules, and it almost always will come as a surprise to your opponent.

TIP
Keep an eye on what your opponent is doing. If he or she is powering up a Benched Pokémon you can assume that it will be Active next.

When you get a Trainer card in your hand, the temptation is to use it right away. But many times the best thing to do is hold on to it for a few turns. Try to use your Trainer cards at times when they will not only help your Pokémon, but also upset your opponent's plans.

For example, if you have a Super Potion card in your hand, it will let you remove up to 4 damage tokens from one of your Pokémon at any point in the game. But if you wait to play that Super Potion until a time when your opponent thinks he or she can Knock Out your Pokémon on the next turn, you will extend your Pokémon's health *and* make your opponent rethink his or her plans. Maybe your Active Pokémon can outslug his or her Active Pokémon and your opponent might have to retreat.

When you play your Trainer cards is at least as important as what effect they have. Trainer cards

Great Card!

Some cards, like Bill, can get more cards in your
hand where you can use them right away!

are one of the ways you have to change the mood of
the game. Make good use of them.

DRAWING CARDS

The danger of using Trainer cards like Bill and
Professor Oak is that they take you one step closer
to losing the game by running out of cards in your
deck. So you need to use these cards carefully in the
later turns of a long game.

But, Bill and Professor Oak are two of the most
powerful Trainer cards in the game. Why? Because
they give you extra cards. And extra cards give you
more Energy, more Pokémon, and more Trainer
cards. Look at what Bill gives you: You put 1 card

(Bill) in your discard pile to draw 2 cards. Where you once had 1 card in your hand, you now have 2. Most decks could use 4 Bills.

There are some basic strategies for when and how to use Bill and Professor Oak. Early in the game, you should always play Bill before you do anything else. Those 2 extra cards may alter your plans for that turn. Later in the game you need to weigh the chance you will run out of cards with the possible benefits of 2 new cards.

Professor Oak is a little harder to play because it makes you discard all the cards you have in your hand before you draw the 7 new cards Professor Oak gives you. The absolute best time to play Professor Oak is when it is the last card in your hand. Now you are trading 1 card (Professor Oak) for 7 new cards. So, if you have any cards in your hand that you can play, play them first and then play Professor Oak. And don't be afraid to discard some Energy this way. Chances are good that you will draw some more Energy in those 7 new cards.

EVOLVING

Choosing which Pokémon to Evolve is a tricky matter. Your final decision will have to do with

TIP
Having lots of cards in your hand is very important. But be careful that you don't draw so many that you run out or you'll lose the game.

which Pokémon you're Evolving and how close the game is to an end. If you have more than one of the needed Basic Pokémon, you should always try to Evolve a Pokémon that has taken less damage. This lets you use the Evolved Pokémon longer. However, sometimes you'll have to Evolve a hurt Pokémon because it is the only way to keep it from getting Knocked Out.

Deciding *when* to Evolve your Pokémon is something that's harder to give advice about. If you have lots of Stage 1 Pokémon, you've probably built a deck that's designed to overwhelm your opponents, so you'll want to Evolve your Pokémon as quickly as possible.

Remember, Evolution might make your Pokémon more powerful, but it can still be used as part of a defensive strategy. For example, if you and your opponent are trading blows with your Active Pokémon in a race to see which one will get Knocked Out first, you can change the conditions of the race by Evolving your Pokémon to give it more Hit Points and bigger attacks.

Of course, you also have to make sure you can power up those bigger attacks. So you might not want to Evolve a Pokémon until you have attached enough Energy to it, so that you can use its new attacks. For more surprise value, attach the last Energy card you need after you Evolve it so you don't give your opponent any advance warning.

RETREATING

Beginners don't think much about Retreat Cost. They just attack with their Pokémon every turn and don't plan too far ahead. But a little experience shows it's a good idea to look at the strongest attack your opponent can use next turn. If that attack would Knock Out your Active Pokémon, then think about retreating.

TIP
Your Bench is more than just a place for your reserve Pokémon. Make sure you're getting at least one Pokémon ready to battle while your Active Pokémon is attacking.

The biggest help retreating gives you is that it will prevent one of your Pokémon from getting Knocked Out. Remember that even if you have plenty of Pokémon on the Bench and your opponent is nowhere close to collecting his or her last Prize, it can still be a good idea to prevent a Knock Out just so your opponent doesn't get to draw a Prize card.

Retreating can also heal your Pokémon from effects like Confusion or Poison. The easier it is for you to get your Pokémon to the Bench, the less you will suffer from attacks like these and others like Sandshrew's Sand-attack (which forces your Pokémon to flip a coin; on tails, your Pokémon's attack fails).

HIT THE BENCH

How do you get your Pokémon back on the Bench? Sometimes your best bet is simply to play a Trainer card (both Switch and Scoop Up work very well). Even if you don't have any Trainer cards in your hand, remember that you can always retreat by paying the Retreat Cost directly.

If you want to be able to switch your Pokémon in and out all the time, you'll want Pokémon with a low retreat Cost—either 1 or 0. Pokémon that cost nothing to retreat are especially useful. If you have one (like Diglett) in your opening hand, play it as your starting Pokémon. When your turn comes around, put the Pokémon you really want to use on your Bench, and retreat your Active Pokémon for free, replacing it with the Benched Pokémon.

In effect, you've seen what Active Pokémon your opponent has chosen before he or she gets to see yours, which can be a big advantage. Plus, if your opponent goes first, your new Active Pokémon won't have any damage yet, putting you back in the lead in the race to the first Knock Out.

MANAGING THE BENCH

In this game the most important thing is the Pokémon you have available to send into the fight. Some players think that means they should put as many different Pokémon as possible on their Bench. This is usually a bad idea.

Only put as many Pokémon as you need out on the Bench at one time. In other words, always have one Pokémon out there, but only add others when they're absolutely necessary. As soon as your opponent sees a new Pokémon on your Bench, he or she can start making plans on how to stop it. And the more you can keep your opponent guessing, the better position you'll have in the game.

It's all about timing.

You need to put your Pokémon down soon enough to give it enough Energy to attack, and enough time to Evolve, but not so soon that you give your opponent an advantage. You must determine how many turns it will take you to power up and Evolve your Pokémon. At the same time, you need to look at the battle that your Active Pokémon is in and decide if you have enough time to get that Pokémon ready.

This is probably the toughest part of the **Pokémon** TCG to master. But once you learn it, you'll find that managing your Bench becomes second nature—you won't even have to think about it, you'll just do it right naturally.

TIP
Combos are cool, but make sure you don't give your opponent an advantage while you wait to set off that cool combo!

COMBOS

When you built your deck, you gave some thought to which

combos you'd be able to use when playing. Part of your strategy should then be to play your cards in a way that lets you use those combos. So, if you have Magnemite ready to Self Destruct but you don't have the Defender card yet, you might want to keep Magnemite on your Bench until you find Defender.

Using a combo may not always be the best thing to do in every game. Combos give you an advantage in the game, but they almost always leave you open to some kind of counter-attack. For example, Magnemite will damage the Pokémon on your Bench when it Self Destructs. Your Opponent might be able to Knock Out one or more of your Benched Pokémon on his or her next turn. As with Trainer cards and Evolution, sometimes the smartest thing to do with a combo is wait.

Also, never stop looking for new combos. Watch what combos your opponent uses. When you see one you like or that was really good, store it away in your mind. Then when you make your next deck, you might be able to build that combo into your new deck.

ENJOYING THE GAME

It might seem silly to talk about fun being part of your strategy, but we think it is as important as which Pokémon you put in your deck. If winning is the only thing that will make a **Pokémon** game fun for you, then you're going to have a lot of unhappy games. Remember that half of the people who play the **Pokémon** TCG every day will not win. So what can you do to make the game more fun whether you win or lose?

Play with friends. It is always easier to have a good time with someone you like. If your opponent is someone you've just met, treat him or her like a friend. It will help make the game fun for both of you.

TIP

Practice playing as often as you can, but don't forget to take a break every now and then to stretch your legs (and your mind).

Take regular breaks. The **Pokémon** trading card game is a lot of fun, but if you sit and play over and over again for hours, it is easy to forget about having fun and worry only about who won the last game. At least once an hour, you should put your cards down and do something else for a few minutes. Get a drink, talk about school, or even trade cards with your friends. It doesn't matter as long as you do some-thing to focus your mind on something other than winning for a few minutes.

Remember the things that worked right. Sometimes your deck just won't give you the cards you need. You'll probably lose more of these games than you win. Play as well as you can, but don't worry about it. There will be times when you get exactly the cards you need. Think about these times rather than dwelling on the troubles you're having just then.

Compliment your opponent. Pay attention to what cards, combos, and strategy your opponent uses. When he or she does something smart, clever, or cool, say something. We all enjoy hearing compliments, and you'll probably find that you like giving them as well.

You'll know you're playing **Pokémon** right when everyone in the game is having a good time and wants to play again. In fact, if you want a cool place to play (and some tips on how to make better trades) take a look now at the next section, where we have some information about the **Pokémon** Trading Card Game League and some great tips for trading.

SECTION THREE

....

VENTURING INTO THE WORLD OF POKÉMON

THE POKÉMON TCG LEAGUE

So NOW YOU KNOW HOW TO PLAY the **Pokémon** trading card game. You have some cards. You even have a couple of decks you like to play. But you're tired of playing against your dad and your little sister. Plus, the whole family has the same cards, so you never find any new cards (and how much fun is it to trade cards with mom?).

You think that you're ready to venture out (with permission from mom and dad) to play **Pokémon** and trade cards outside of the house. But you still need a little help. In this section of the book, we're going to tell you about a great place where you can go play **Pokémon** and get some help to become the best Pokémon trainer you can be.

We'll also give you some tips about how to collect, organize, and trade your **Pokémon** cards safely, so you can build your collection without worrying about damaging or losing your cards. We've even put together some cool lists that can help you keep track of all your cards. The last chapter is a set of questions and answers about the **Pokémon** TCG. So if you still have questions after reading this book, take a look at the "Frequently Asked Questions" chapter.

But first, let's talk about that cool place to play.

JOIN THE LEAGUE

There's a place near you where you can meet new friends who also play the **Pokémon** TCG, play games with them, trade cards, and even win cool stuff like cards, stickers, and badges (just like Ash). This cool place is called the **Pokémon** Trading Card Game League. You even get cool stuff just for joining, and you earn points by participating. The more points you earn, the more great stuff you can get.

COOL STUFF!
You'll get cool stuff just for joining the **Pokémon** TCG League like badges and promo cards.

This chapter has everything you need to know to get started. You'll find out what you get just for joining, where you can find a **Pokémon** TCG League center near you, and how to earn points. You'll also find a glossary to help you understand what everyone's talking about at the League center. We'll show you how to keep track of your points, all the badges you can earn, and what else you get for earning points.

As we're writing this book, the second League season is almost ready to start. Trainers (that's what you're called when you join the **Pokémon** TCG League) who joined the League in January got a free Mew card! This card was not available anywhere else! That's the kind of cool stuff we're talking about. If you join the League and play in league events, you could earn even more cool stuff.

GETTING STARTED

First, you need to find a **Pokémon** TCG League center. Wizards of the Coast is always looking for more locations. Right now you can find a League center at the following stores.

- All Wizards of the Coast stores
- All Books-a-Million stores
- All Zany Brainy stores
- All Toys 'R' Us stores
- Select Game Keeper stores
- Select Borders Books and Music stores
- Select hobby game retail stores

More League centers may have opened since we wrote this book. For the latest list, go to www.wizards.com/Pokemon. Here, you're sure to find a Pokémon TCG League center near you.

Once you find a **Pokémon** TCG League center, joining is simple. You just go to the League center when there's a League event going on (these are usually on the weekend during the afternoon). All **Pokémon** TCG League centers have a schedule of events so you can go into the store to see when the next event will happen and then just show up.

Events can be anywhere from two to four hours long and are usually the same day every week. Some League centers could have more than one League event a week, or even more than one a day!

When you get there, you'll want to find the Gym Leader. He or she will tell you what you need to do to become a member of the **Pokémon** TCG League. The most important step is to fill out your **Pokémon** DCI membership card. Have your mom or dad help you. And if mom or dad have any questions about the form, the Gym Leader can answer them. You'll need to fill in all the information on the form. Make sure you fill it out clearly. This information is used only to set up your membership, and you can use your DCI number to look up your own personal page at www.wizards.com/Pokemon.

Once you fill out your DCI mem-

TIP
The **Pokémon** TCG League is a cool place where you can play **Pokémon** and trade cards every week.

bership card, you'll get a **Pokémon** TCG League badge book to keep track of your points. You are now ready to start earning some points. If you just can't wait any longer, go ahead and play a couple of games. Just make sure you let the Gym Leader know you're playing a game. This way, you'll be sure to get your points.

LEAGUE GLOSSARY

Now, before we talk about how to use the League badge book you just got, we'd like to show you some of the words and phrases you will hear at the **Pokémon** TCG League so you can learn what they mean. Below are some of the most common words and phrases and their meanings. Browse through it now. Then you can always come back if you hear something you don't quite understand.

Activity—There are six different activities, one for each week of the season. Trainers can earn points for completing them. Activities are like word searches, storytelling, or drawing.

Badge Book—A badge book is used to keep track of all the points a trainer earns during the season. We discuss how to use the badge book a little later.

Certified Coach Sticker—Trainers earn this sticker when they pass the Coach's test. It goes on the back cover of the trainer's badge book. Certified Coaches can earn points by teaching other League members how to play the **Pokémon** TCG.

Coach Test—To become a Certified Coach, trainers must take a 15-question Coach's test. You need to get 13 or more right out of 15 to earn your Certified Coach sticker.

DCI Membership Card—To become an official trainer, your Gym Leader needs to see your DCI membership card. If you don't have one, your Gym Leader will give you one. You can use your DCI number to check out your own personal page at <u>www.wizards.com/Pokemon</u>.

Gym Leader—The Gym Leader helps trainers reach their goals by leading them through the session's activities. They pair up trainers to play against each other, hand out League activities, and stamp badge books as trainers earn points. You can identify the Gym Leader by his or her bright yellow shirt.

Season—Each **Pokémon** TCG League season is six weeks long. Like Ash's travels in the Pokémon animated series, the **Pokémon** TCG League seasons take trainers to various "Gyms." The eight seasons, in order, are: Pewter City, Cerulean City, Vermilion City, Celadon City, Saffron City, Fuchsia City, Cinnabar Island, and Viridian City.

Session—A two- to four-hour block of time set aside by the

TIP
Your badge book helps you track your points as you complete activities. Don't lose it.

League center for trainers to earn points for teaching and playing games, trading, and completing League activities.

Stamp—Gym Leaders use stamps to mark trainers' badge books when they earn points in the League.

TM Sticker—"Technical Machines" have hints on how to play better. They are awarded when a trainer earns 700 and 900 points. Your badge book has special pages for TM stickers.

Trainer Badge—Trainers can earn eight different badges, one in each season. When a trainer reaches 500 points, he or she earns the badge for that season. They are: Boulder, Cascade, Thunder, Rainbow, Marsh, Soul, Volcano, and Earth. Don't worry, if you don't get enough points in one season, you can continue working on a badge during the next season before starting to work on your next badge.

Trainer—A participant in the **Pokémon** TCG League. The League calls all members trainers (because you're not a Master yet).

YOUR BADGE BOOK

So, now you have your badge book and you're ready to earn points on your way to your first badge. But what is this badge book anyway and how do you use it?

Like we said earlier, each season is six weeks long. During the season there will be some things

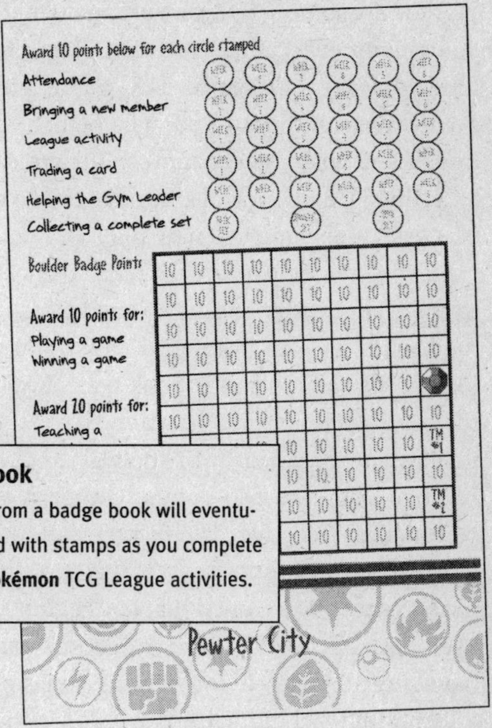

Award 10 points below for each circle stamped

Attendance

Bringing a new member

League activity

Trading a card

Helping the Gym Leader

Collecting a complete set

Boulder Badge Points

Award 10 points for:
Playing a game
Winning a game

Award 20 points for:
Teaching a

Badge Book

This page from a badge book will eventually be filled with stamps as you complete different **Pokémon** TCG League activities.

Pewter City

you can do once each week to earn points (like just showing up or trading a card). The Gym Leader will mark those circles in your badge book with a stamp to show that you earned points that week for that activity. He or she will also mark one of the squares in the point grid at the bottom of the page. Each of these squares is worth 10 points.

There are some activities you can do that will earn you points every time you complete them. Each time you play a **Pokémon** TCG game, you earn 10 points. You get those 10 points whether you win or lose. If you win, you get another 10 points! If you're a Certified Coach, you also earn 20 points each time you teach the game to a new player.

As you complete activities, take your badge book to the Gym Leader and he or she will fill in one of the squares in your point grid with a stamp. Take a look at the sample badge book page. See how each row of your point grid has 10 boxes? So each row that's stamped is worth 100 points.

When you earn 500 points, you earn the badge pictured on the page. The badges are a neat metal pin that you can put on your jacket or your backpack to show you earned that badge! If you want to keep earning points after you get the badge (and have some time left in the season), you can work for a Technical Machine (TM). The TMs are stickers that give you strategy tips for playing the **Pokémon** TCG. You earn TMs at 700 and 900 points.

Each page in your badge book represents one season. Each season is named after a city that Ash and his friends visited while he was earning his eight Trainer badges on the way to joining the Pokémon League in the story. Those cities and badges are:

Pewter City
Gym Leader:
Brock
Favorite Pokémon:
Fighting (Rock)
Badge: Boulder

Saffron City
Gym Leader:
Sabrina
Favorite Pokémon:
Psychic
Badge: Marsh

Cerulean City
Gym Leader:
Misty
Favorite Pokémon:
Water
Badge: Cascade

Fuchsia City
Gym Leader:
Koga
Favorite Pokémon: Grass
(Poison)
Badge: Soul

Vermilion City
Gym Leader:
Lt. Surge
Favorite Pokémon:
Lightning
Badge: Thunder

Cinnabar Island
Gym Leader:
Blaine
Favorite Pokémon: Fire
Badge: Volcano

Celadon City
Gym Leader:
Erika
Favorite Pokémon:
Grass
Badge: Rainbow

Viridian City
Gym Leader:
Giovanni
Favorite Pokémon:
Fighting (Ground)
Badge: Earth

EARNING POINTS

We talked a little bit about how you earn points in the last section. Here we will show you all the ways you can earn points. These are all fun things you'll want to do anyway when you get together with your Pokémon friends, so you'll be able to earn 500 points in a snap. Here are the ways that you can earn points:

Attendance—You get 10 points just for showing up each week. You can earn these points only once per week.

Bring a New Member—You get 10 points if you bring a friend who signs up for the League. You can earn these points only once per week.

League Activities—Every week, the League center will have a new, totally fun League activity for you. These might be puzzles or a picture to color. When you complete the activity, you earn 10 points. You can earn these points only once per week.

Trade a Card—Once per week, you get 10 points for trading a **Pokémon** TCG card. You can trade any cards you want, but you won't get extra points for trading more than one card. You can earn these points only once per week (and you can't get points for trading basic Energy cards).

Help the Gym Leader—Each Gym Leader will have different guidelines for what he or she needs help with. But don't be afraid to ask your Gym Leader if you can help out. If you do help the Gym Leader, you'll get 10 points.

Collect a Complete Set—Once per season, you get 10 points for each different complete set of **Pokémon** TCG cards you collect. For example, if you have a complete set of *Jungle* cards *and* a complete set of *Fossil* cards, you can get 20 total points for those sets *each* season!

TIP
Every point you earn takes you one step closer to getting your badge, so make sure the Gym Leader knows when you complete an activity.

Play a Game—For each game of **Pokémon** you play, you get 10 points. Even if you don't win the game, you still get those points. You could play 10 games, and even if you don't win a single one, you still get 100 points! That's one whole row of boxes.

Win a Game—For each game you win, you get another 10 points. Don't be disappointed if you don't win every game. Sometimes you play your best and your friend still wins. Just think of these 10 points as a bonus for playing extra well!

Teach a New Player—Before you can teach others how to play, you need to take the Coach's test and answer at least 13 out of 15 questions correctly. Once you are a Certified Coach, you can earn 20 points for teaching a new player how to play the game!

Remember, there are plenty of ways to get points. You don't have to win a lot of games. If you show up every week with a new friend, trade a card, and complete an activity, you'll earn 240 points in that season! You're almost halfway toward your badge without even playing a game!

CONTINUING YOUR LEAGUE ADVENTURE

Now you know everything you need to know to get started in the League. We think you'll enjoy the experience and we know your parents will appreciate the atmosphere of the League centers, which offer a safe place to play and are geared toward having fun, not just competing.

Now, let us give you trainers one final piece of advice. We've said this several times already in this book: Have fun. The **Pokémon** TCG League is a great place to go make new friends, play **Pokémon** and trade cards, try out some cool activities, and earn cool stuff. But you won't enjoy yourself if all you worry about is winning every game. That's not what the League is all about. It's about having fun and playing a game you love with your friends.

CATCHING EM ALL

ONE OF THE MOST REWARDING THINGS about **Pokémon** is the ability to "catch 'em all." In fact, in the last chapter we told you how you could earn points in the **Pokémon** Trading Card Game League by collecting a complete set of cards and by trading cards during a League event. Well, these two activities are related to each other. To collect all the **Pokémon** TCG cards, you will have to trade cards with your friends (unless your parents buy lots and lots of cards).

It's actually a lot more fun to trade cards than to just "buy" your way to a set. But collecting and trading are hard to do and harder to do right. So, in this chapter, we will give you some advice and some tools to help you "catch 'em all" easily and "keep 'em all" safe.

KNOW THE RULES

There are actually many different **Pokémon** TCG cards, so there's more to collect than just the 151 Pokémon. For example, there's more than one card called "Pikachu." In fact we know of four different English language Pikachus—Base Set, *Jungle*, promo card 1, and promo card 4. With all the different abilities some Pokémon have, you need three or four cards to cover them all! Don't forget Trainer and Energy cards, too.

Before you can collect anything—especially trading card game cards—you need to understand certain rules about them. How do you get them? What makes one card different from another? How do you know when you have all of them? How do you make a good trade? We'll try to answer these questions (and some you might not have thought to ask) as we lay down the rules for you.

GETTING CARDS

Pokémon TCG cards come in several different kinds of packaging. Each one has a different selection of cards. Below is a general breakdown of what you'll get in starter sets, theme decks, and booster packs.

Starter Sets come with two decks of 30 cards

each, a rulebook, a foil coin, damage counters, and a special holofoil card. Each Starter Set contains the same 61 cards. Of the 61 cards, 3 of them are rare cards, 16 are uncommon cards, and the other 42 are common cards.

Theme Decks, like the Starter Set, contain 60 cards, a rulebook, a foil coin, and damage counters. Unlike Starter Sets, there is no 61st card. But you still get one holofoil card in each theme deck (it's already part of the deck).

Of the 60 cards in a theme deck, 3 of them are rare cards, 15 are uncommon cards, and the other 42 are common cards. Although there are several different kinds of theme decks (each with a different name), each theme deck with the same name will always have the same 60 cards.

Booster Packs are the smallest type of packaging, but the most important for building your collection. They contain 11 randomly assorted **Pokémon** TCG cards. Each pack contains 1 rare card, 3 uncommon cards, and 7 common cards. Although the rarity distribution is fixed, the exact cards you get of each rarity is random. So, each time you buy a booster pack you get a different group of 11 cards from the set.

TIP
There are three ways to buy **Pokémon** cards: Starter Sets, Theme Decks, and Booster Packs. For collecting, booster packs are the way to go.

RARITY

Not all **Pokémon** TCG cards are printed in equal numbers. There are 4 basic kinds of rarity—common, uncommon, rare, and rare holofoil. You can tell whether a card is common, uncommon, or rare by looking at the bottom right-hand corner of the card. After the card number, you will see a symbol—either ●, ◆, or ★. Common cards have a ●, uncommon cards a ◆, and rare cards a ★. Energy Removal, for instance, is a common. It has "92/102 ●" printed on the bottom right-hand corner of the card.

So what does that rarity mean? An easy way to remember the difference between rarities is to look at the cards in a booster pack. A booster pack has 7 common cards. That's more than half the pack! Like their name, common cards are the easiest cards to collect. A booster pack also has 3 uncommon cards and 1 rare card.

So, if you look at the cards in a booster pack, you can see that there are 7 times as many total common cards as rare cards and 3 times as many total uncommon cards as rare cards.

Holofoil cards are a special kind of rare card. There are even fewer holofoil cards than there are other rare cards. They have a special foil coating that makes them reflect light in really cool patterns. There are about 2 times as many total regular rare cards as there are holofoil cards. (You should get about 1 holofoil rare card per 3 packs you open).

Once you see how the rarities work, you begin to understand why you never want to trade a rare card for a common card. We'll talk more about trading later in this chapter. The one exception to the rarity structure is promotional cards. They are typically given away—like the four cards from *Pokémon: The First Movie*—usually one per customer to help promote both the **Pokémon** TCG and other **Pokémon** products. We'll also talk more about these later.

BASE SETS AND EXPANSIONS

The other obstacle in your quest to "catch 'em all" is telling the difference between sets of cards. **Pokémon** TCG cards are printed in sets. There have been four sets so far—two versions of the Base Set, the *Jungle* set, and the *Fossil* set. The *Team Rocket* set will be coming out soon.

There are two editions of the basic set, which is where you get a lot of the different Pokémon, most of your Trainer cards, and all of your Basic Energy cards. Base Set 2 is the most recent basic set. Wizards of the Coast releases new basic sets to give people a chance to see some of the cards that were released in other sets after those sets are out of

TIP
There are over 200 different **Pokémon** TCG cards now. Collecting by sets gives you an easy way to break down your collection into manageable chunks.

print.

Base Set 2 has most of the cards from the original Base Set plus lots of cards from the *Jungle* set that was released last year. To tell the difference between the original Base Set and Base Set 2, look for the Base Set 2 icon on the cards. The original Base Set had no icon.

Base Set: No Icon

Base Set 2:

Expansion sets usually have a theme associated with them. *Jungle*, the first expansion set, contained many Grass Pokémon. All *Jungle* cards have a palm tree icon. *Fossil*, the second expansion set, revolved around different prehistoric Pokémon that you could evolve from Mysterious Fossils. All *Fossil* cards have a skeleton foot icon.

Team Rocket, the next expansion set, will have Pokémon trained by those "bad boys" of Pokémon—Team Rocket. All *Team Rocket* cards will have the Team Rocket "R" icon.

Jungle set:

Fossil set:

1st Edition cards add another way to collect **Pokémon** cards. You can tell a 1st Edition card by the special symbol printed on the card. Only a limited number of 1st Edition cards are printed for each set. Once they're gone, you can't get them anymore because Wizards of the Coast won't print any more. These 1st Edition cards are for hardcore collectors. Unlimited cards (with no 1st Edition symbol) are identical in every way to 1st Edition cards, except they don't have the 1st Edition symbol.

1st Edition cards:

PROMOTIONAL CARDS

You may be wondering, "What is a promo card?" These are cards printed specially for a promotion. Some promo cards have the Promo Star icon. These cards were never released in one of the sets. They were only printed for special promotions. For example, Wizards of the Coast worked with Warner Brothers to provide promo cards for *Pokémon: The First Movie* last November.

These cards (the ones with the promo star) are completely new cards with different art and different abilities on the card. A card with the promo star has a single collector number: A numeral 4 in the corner shows it is the fourth card so far with the promo star. As more promo cards are printed, this number will get larger.

Other promo cards, like the gold-bordered Meowth in Fruit by the Foot or the foil-stamped cards in *TopDeck* magazine from time to time, are simply reprints of existing cards with something special

TIP
A lot of the **Pokémon** TCG promo cards are given out through the **Pokémon** TCG League.

added to make them look cool. These cards never have the promo star on them and they have the same collector number they had when they were first printed.

Promo cards aren't necessarily rarer than cards printed in the sets (it depends on the print run of the card and the success of the promotion). But both the completely new cards and the reprinted cards with special borders or foil stamps all share one thing in common: the only way to get these promo cards is through the promotion. If you miss the promotion, you miss the card.

ENOUGH IS ENOUGH

Once you start collecting **Pokémon** TCG cards, you may want to put a limit on how many you want of a certain card. If you want to keep these cards in a set for a long time, you'll want enough copies of each card to have a complete set—1 of each card—and still have some cards to build decks to play with (if you're a player as well).

Since your deck can have only up to 4 cards with the same name on it, if you're both a player and a collector, you may want to have 4 of each card in your play binder plus the 1 in your collection binder. So, at most you will need 5 of each **Pokémon** TCG card.

To make it easier on yourself, you may also want to think about how many of each card you are really likely to play with. You can go though the cards in a set and determine how many you will need. For some cards, like Bill and Professor Oak, you may want a couple in every deck, so you may need more than 4. But you probably don't need more than 1 or 2 Stage 2 Pokémon in a deck, so 2 in your play binder should be plenty.

PROTECT YOUR CARDS

Once you start collecting a lot of **Pokémon** TCG cards, you need some system for storing them. There are several ways for you to keep your **Pokémon** TCG cards from getting dinged, worn out, or bent. Whether you're playing with them or putting them in a box or in a binder, there are products made especially for trading card game cards.

Binders are available in all varieties and are the best way to store cards if you want to look at them quickly. There are even binders made specifically for carrying **Pokémon** TCG cards. Binders come in four- and nine-pocket varieties, and can be two- or three-ring binders or prebound books. Binders are ideal for collecting and trading because they allow you to look at many cards at once without having to handle them. That saves a lot of wear and tear on your cards.

TIP
Special card sleeves are made for trading card game cards. These protect your cards *and* allow you to shuffle the cards easily.

The most economical way to protect your cards is in a box. There are specially designed boxes just for trading cards, and they're typically less than a dollar each. These can hold hundreds of cards in a small space. You can also get larger boxes that can hold thousands of cards for a few dollars more. You can even stack these to keep huge collections together. Once again, you can also get boxes specifically made for **Pokémon** TCG cards. Boxes are a great investment for the rest of your collection after building complete sets and putting them in binders.

WHAT MAKES A FAIR TRADE?

We'll start with the most basic information. Know your rarities. We discussed these earlier, so we won't go over them again, but the first rule of trading is to make sure that you get the same rarity of card in return for each card you trade. Maybe your friend wants your Super Potion, which is an uncommon card. Your friend should be willing to give you an uncommon card in exchange.

HOW DO I TRADE FOR DIFFERENT RARITIES?

Sometimes you and your friends can't trade a rare for a rare or a common for a common. For example, your friend might not have any uncommon cards to give you for your Super Potion. What should you do then? How many common cards is an uncommon card worth? Without going into confusing details, here's what you should normally expect:

- Each holofoil card should normally be worth 2 to 3 rare cards.
- Each rare card should normally be worth 2 to 3 uncommon cards.
- Each uncommon card should normally be worth 2 to 3 common cards.

TIP
There are twice as many common cards as uncommon cards in a booster pack, so uncommon cards are worth twice as much as common cards.

WHAT ELSE CAN AFFECT A TRADE?

Other things can affect the value of a card. For example, Pokémon that are popular on the animated show or in the Nintendo Game Boy game are often worth more than cards that are less popular. Pikachu is a good example. Many people will give you two or three other common cards in exchange for a single, common Pikachu.

Cards with Basic, Stage 1, or Stage 2 Pokémon on them tend to be worth more than Trainer cards because you have to have Pokémon to play the game, but you don't need Trainers. Some people also care more about "catching" all the Pokémon than the Trainers.

WHY DO YOU WANT THE CARD?

The reason that *you* want a card will also affect how valuable it is to you. People who just want to collect a complete set of **Pokémon** cards are more likely to trade one card for one card. If they have an extra copy of a card, it isn't doing them any good (because they already "caught" that one). So they are more than happy to trade their extra card for a card they need to finish their set.

However, people who are trading to build a better **Pokémon** deck are influenced by whether the card you have is one that they need for their deck. Things like the Pokémon's type and Pokémon Power are big concerns for them. You might be able to get an uncommon card from someone for a really good common card like Bill if that person needs an extra Bill for his or her latest deck. You might even be able to get a rare card from someone for a really good uncommon card like Professor Oak.

CHECK THE CONDITION

You should also keep in mind that cards in good condition are worth more than cards that are worn, bent, or damaged.

- A card in perfect condition, fresh out of the booster pack, is worth the most. This type of card is said to be in mint condition.

- A card that you've played with once or twice, or a card with a nick or two on the edge, is worth slightly less. Those cards are in near mint condition, because they are nearly as good as mint, but not quite.

● A card that is a little bit warped from shuffling, or a card with several nicks or indentations, is said to be in excellent condition.

Most collectors aren't interested in cards that are in anything less than excellent condition. For a true collector, cards in mint condition are often worth twice as much as cards that are in excellent condition—even though most people can't tell them apart! But for a player, cards in excellent condition are just as valuable. A player can often get very good trades from a collector by offering his or her mint cards in exchange for the collector's excellent cards. Both sides get what they want!

CHECK THE PRICE

You may also want to consult a price guide before you do any trading. These can tell you (in very general terms only) the value of the cards involved in the trade. Many magazines that talk about the **Pokémon** TCG have price guides. The listed prices are usually an average of what those cards are selling for in stores across the country.

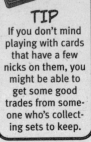

TIP
If you don't mind playing with cards that have a few nicks on them, you might be able to get some good trades from someone who's collecting sets to keep.

Instead of following the price guide to the cent, compare the prices of cards you're looking for to the prices of the cards you're willing to trade away. Remember that the listed prices are national averages. Some cards may be worth more or less in your area. But, you should try to keep the value of the trade even. You normally don't want to trade a card that your price guide says is worth $30 for a card that is worth $1.

CARD LISTS

Of course, the last tool you need to help you complete your collection is a card list, so you can check off what cards you have and know what cards you still need. The next chapter gives you that tool for all the sets that have been released, plus all the promo cards that are out there.

11

POKÉMON CARD CHECK LIST

IF YOU TRULY FEEL YOU HAVE TO "CATCH 'EM ALL" then you need some way to keep track of all the cards that have been printed. In the next few pages, we have supplied a check list for all the sets that Wizards of the Coast has printed so far.

This includes both of the "regular" sets—Base Set (which was printed in 1999) and Base Set 2 (which should be in stores now and replaces Base Set). It also includes the two expansion sets that were printed in 1999—the *Jungle* set and the *Fossil* set— plus all the promotional cards.

To use this check list, simply put an "X" or a check mark in the box in front of the card's name once you have that card in your collection. Card rarity is shown with the symbols. A gray star is used to show holofoils.

BASE SET

• • • • • • • • • • • • • •

- ❑ 1/102 ★ Alakazam
- ❑ 2/102 ★ Blastoise
- ❑ 3/102 ★ Chansey
- ❑ 4/102 ★ Charizard
- ❑ 5/102 ★ Clefairy
- ❑ 6/102 ★ Gyarados
- ❑ 7/102 ★ Hitmonchan
- ❑ 8/102 ★ Machamp
- ❑ 9/102 ★ Magneton
- ❑ 10/102 ★ Mewtwo
- ❑ 11/102 ★ Nidoking
- ❑ 12/102 ★ Ninetales
- ❑ 13/102 ★ Poliwrath
- ❑ 14/102 ★ Raichu
- ❑ 15/102 ★ Venusaur
- ❑ 16/102 ★ Zapdos
- ❑ 17/102 ★ Beedrill
- ❑ 18/102 ★ Dragonair
- ❑ 19/102 ★ Dugtrio
- ❑ 20/102 ★ Electabuzz
- ❑ 21/102 ★ Electrode
- ❑ 22/102 ★ Pidgeotto
- ❑ 23/102 ◆ Arcanine
- ❑ 24/102 ◆ Charmeleon
- ❑ 25/102 ◆ Dewgong
- ❑ 26/102 ◆ Dratini
- ❑ 27/102 ◆ Farfetch'd
- ❑ 28/102 ◆ Growlithe
- ❑ 29/102 ◆ Haunter
- ❑ 30/102 ◆ Ivysaur
- ❑ 31/102 ◆ Jynx
- ❑ 32/102 ◆ Kadabra
- ❑ 33/102 ◆ Kakuna

- ❑ 34/102 ◆ Machoke
- ❑ 35/102 ◆ Magikarp
- ❑ 36/102 ◆ Magmar
- ❑ 37/102 ◆ Nidorino
- ❑ 38/102 ◆ Poliwhirl
- ❑ 39/102 ◆ Porygon
- ❑ 40/102 ◆ Raticate
- ❑ 41/102 ◆ Seel
- ❑ 42/102 ◆ Wartortle
- ❑ 43/102 ● Abra
- ❑ 44/102 ● Bulbasaur
- ❑ 45/102 ● Caterpie
- ❑ 46/102 ● Charmander
- ❑ 47/102 ● Diglett
- ❑ 48/102 ● Doduo
- ❑ 49/102 ● Drowzee
- ❑ 50/102 ● Gastly
- ❑ 51/102 ● Koffing
- ❑ 52/102 ● Machop
- ❑ 53/102 ● Magnemite
- ❑ 54/102 ● Metapod
- ❑ 55/102 ● Nidoran ♂
- ❑ 56/102 ● Onix
- ❑ 57/102 ● Pidgey
- ❑ 58/102 ● Pikachu
- ❑ 59/102 ● Poliwag
- ❑ 60/102 ● Ponyta
- ❑ 61/102 ● Rattata
- ❑ 62/102 ● Sandshrew
- ❑ 63/102 ● Squirtle
- ❑ 64/102 ● Starmie
- ❑ 65/102 ● Staryu
- ❑ 66/102 ● Tangela
- ❑ 67/102 ● Voltorb
- ❑ 68/102 ● Vulpix
- ❑ 69/102 ● Weedle
- ❑ 70/102 ★ Clefairy Doll

- ❏ 71/102 ★ Computer Search
- ❏ 72/102 ★ Devolution Spray
- ❏ 73/102 ★ Imposter Professor Oak
- ❏ 74/102 ★ Item Finder
- ❏ 75/102 ★ Lass
- ❏ 76/102 ★ Pokémon Breeder
- ❏ 77/102 ★ Pokémon Trader
- ❏ 78/102 ★ Scoop Up
- ❏ 79/102 ★ Super Energy Removal
- ❏ 80/102 ◆ Defender
- ❏ 81/102 ◆ Energy Retrieval
- ❏ 82/102 ◆ Full Heal
- ❏ 83/102 ◆ Maintenance
- ❏ 84/102 ◆ PlusPower
- ❏ 85/102 ◆ Pokémon Center
- ❏ 86/102 ◆ Pokémon Flute
- ❏ 87/102 ◆ Pokédex
- ❏ 88/102 ◆ Professor Oak
- ❏ 89/102 ◆ Revive
- ❏ 90/102 ◆ Super Potion
- ❏ 91/102 ● Bill
- ❏ 92/102 ● Energy Removal
- ❏ 93/102 ● Gust of Wind
- ❏ 94/102 ● Potion
- ❏ 95/102 ● Switch

- ❏ 96/102 ● Double Colorless Energy
- ❏ 97/102 ● Fighting Energy
- ❏ 98/102 ● Fire Energy
- ❏ 99/102 ● Grass Energy
- ❏ 100/102 ● Lightning Energy
- ❏ 101/102 ● Psychic Energy
- ❏ 102/102 ● Water Energy

BASE SET 2

• • • • • • • • • • • • • • • •

- ❏ 1/130 ★ Alakazam
- ❏ 2/130 ★ Blastoise
- ❏ 3/130 ★ Chansey
- ❏ 4/130 ★ Charizard
- ❏ 5/130 ★ Clefable
- ❏ 6/130 ★ Clefairy
- ❏ 7/130 ★ Gyarados
- ❏ 8/130 ★ Hitmonchan
- ❏ 9/130 ★ Magneton
- ❏ 10/130 ★ Mewtwo
- ❏ 11/130 ★ Nidoking
- ❏ 12/130 ★ Nidoqueen
- ❏ 13/130 ★ Ninetales
- ❏ 14/130 ★ Pidgeot
- ❏ 15/130 ★ Poliwrath

- ❏ 16/130 ★ Raichu
- ❏ 17/130 ★ Scyther
- ❏ 18/130 ★ Venusaur
- ❏ 19/130 ★ Wigglytuff
- ❏ 20/130 ★ Zapdos
- ❏ 21/130 ★ Beedrill
- ❏ 22/130 ★ Dragonair
- ❏ 23/130 ★ Dugtrio
- ❏ 24/130 ★ Electabuzz
- ❏ 25/130 ★ Electrode
- ❏ 26/130 ★ Kangaskhan
- ❏ 27/130 ★ Mr. Mime
- ❏ 28/130 ★ Pidgeotto
- ❏ 29/130 ★ Pinsir
- ❏ 30/130 ★ Snorlax
- ❏ 31/130 ★ Venomoth
- ❏ 32/130 ★ Victreebel
- ❏ 33/130 ◆ Arcanine
- ❏ 34/130 ◆ Butterfree
- ❏ 35/130 ◆ Charmeleon
- ❏ 36/130 ◆ Dewgong
- ❏ 37/130 ◆ Dodrio
- ❏ 38/130 ◆ Dratini
- ❏ 39/130 ◆ Exeggutor
- ❏ 40/130 ◆ Farfetch'd
- ❏ 41/130 ◆ Fearow
- ❏ 42/130 ◆ Growlithe
- ❏ 43/130 ◆ Haunter
- ❏ 44/130 ◆ Ivysaur
- ❏ 45/130 ◆ Jynx
- ❏ 46/130 ◆ Kadabra
- ❏ 47/130 ◆ Kakuna
- ❏ 48/130 ◆ Lickitung
- ❏ 49/130 ◆ Machoke
- ❏ 50/130 ◆ Magikarp
- ❏ 51/130 ◆ Magmar
- ❏ 52/130 ◆ Marowak
- ❏ 53/130 ◆ Nidorina
- ❏ 54/130 ◆ Nidorino
- ❏ 55/130 ◆ Parasect
- ❏ 56/130 ◆ Persian
- ❏ 57/130 ◆ Poliwhirl
- ❏ 58/130 ◆ Raticate
- ❏ 59/130 ◆ Rhydon
- ❏ 60/130 ◆ Seaking
- ❏ 61/130 ◆ Seel
- ❏ 62/130 ◆ Tauros
- ❏ 63/130 ◆ Wartortle
- ❏ 64/130 ◆ Weepinbell
- ❏ 65/130 ● Abra
- ❏ 66/130 ● Bellsprout
- ❏ 67/130 ● Bulbasaur
- ❏ 68/130 ● Caterpie
- ❏ 69/130 ● Charmander
- ❏ 70/130 ● Cubone
- ❏ 71/130 ● Diglett
- ❏ 72/130 ● Doduo
- ❏ 73/130 ● Drowzee
- ❏ 74/130 ● Exeggcute
- ❏ 75/130 ● Gastly
- ❏ 76/130 ● Goldeen
- ❏ 77/130 ● Jigglypuff
- ❏ 78/130 ● Machop
- ❏ 79/130 ● Magnemite
- ❏ 80/130 ● Meowth
- ❏ 81/130 ● Metapod
- ❏ 82/130 ● Nidoran ♀
- ❏ 83/130 ● Nidoran ♂
- ❏ 84/130 ● Onix
- ❏ 85/130 ● Paras
- ❏ 86/130 ● Pidgey
- ❏ 87/130 ● Pikachu
- ❏ 88/130 ● Poliwag
- ❏ 89/130 ● Rattata

❑ 90/130 ● Rhyhorn
❑ 91/130 ● Sandshrew
❑ 92/130 ● Spearow
❑ 93/130 ● Squirtle
❑ 94/130 ● Starmie
❑ 95/130 ● Staryu
❑ 96/130 ● Tangela
❑ 97/130 ● Venonat
❑ 98/130 ● Voltorb
❑ 99/130 ● Vulpix
❑ 100/130 ● Weedle
❑ 101/130 ★ Computer Search
❑ 102/130 ★ Imposter Professor Oak
❑ 103/130 ★ Item Finder
❑ 104/130 ★ Lass
❑ 105/130 ★ Pokémon Breeder
❑ 106/130 ★ Pokémon Trader
❑ 107/130 ★ Scoop Up
❑ 108/130 ★ Super Energy Removal
❑ 109/130 ◆ Defender
❑ 110/130 ◆ Energy Retrieval
❑ 111/130 ◆ Full Heal
❑ 112/130 ◆ Maintenance
❑ 113/130 ◆ PlusPower
❑ 114/130 ◆ Pokémon Center
❑ 115/130 ◆ Pokédex
❑ 116/130 ◆ Professor Oak
❑ 117/130 ◆ Super Potion

❑ 118/130 ● Bill
❑ 119/130 ● Energy Removal
❑ 120/130 ● Gust of Wind
❑ 121/130 ● Poké Ball
❑ 122/130 ● Potion
❑ 123/130 ● Switch
❑ 124/130 ● Double Colorless Energy
❑ 125/130 Fighting Energy
❑ 126/130 Fire Energy
❑ 127/130 Grass Energy
❑ 128/130 Lightning Energy
❑ 129/130 Psychic Energy
❑ 130/130 Water Energy

JUNGLE

●●●●●●●●●●●

❑ 1/64 ★ Clefable
❑ 2/64 ★ Electrode
❑ 3/64 ★ Flareon
❑ 4/64 ★ Jolteon
❑ 5/64 ★ Kangaskhan
❑ 6/64 ★ Mr. Mime
❑ 7/64 ★ Nidoqueen
❑ 8/64 ★ Pidgeot
❑ 9/64 ★ Pinsir
❑ 10/64 ★ Scyther

- ❑ 11/64 ★ Snorlax
- ❑ 12/64 ★ Vaporeon
- ❑ 13/64 ★ Venomoth
- ❑ 14/64 ★ Victreebel
- ❑ 15/64 ★ Vileplume
- ❑ 16/64 ★ Wigglytuff
- ❑ 17/64 ★ Clefable
- ❑ 18/64 ★ Electrode
- ❑ 19/64 ★ Flareon
- ❑ 20/64 ★ Jolteon
- ❑ 21/64 ★ Kangaskhan
- ❑ 22/64 ★ Mr. Mime
- ❑ 23/64 ★ Nidoqueen
- ❑ 24/64 ★ Pidgeot
- ❑ 25/64 ★ Pinsir
- ❑ 26/64 ★ Scyther
- ❑ 27/64 ★ Snorlax
- ❑ 28/64 ★ Vaporeon
- ❑ 29/64 ★ Venomoth
- ❑ 30/64 ★ Victreebel
- ❑ 31/64 ★ Vileplume
- ❑ 32/64 ★ Wigglytuff
- ❑ 33/64 ◆ Butterfree
- ❑ 34/64 ◆ Dodrio
- ❑ 35/64 ◆ Exeggutor
- ❑ 36/64 ◆ Fearow
- ❑ 37/64 ◆ Gloom
- ❑ 38/64 ◆ Lickitung
- ❑ 39/64 ◆ Marowak
- ❑ 40/64 ◆ Nidorina
- ❑ 41/64 ◆ Parasect
- ❑ 42/64 ◆ Persian
- ❑ 43/64 ◆ Primeape
- ❑ 44/64 ◆ Rapidash
- ❑ 45/64 ◆ Rhydon
- ❑ 46/64 ◆ Seaking
- ❑ 47/64 ◆ Tauros

- ❑ 48/64 ◆ Weepinbell
- ❑ 49/64 ● Bellsprout
- ❑ 50/64 ● Cubone
- ❑ 51/64 ● Eevee
- ❑ 52/64 ● Exeggcute
- ❑ 53/64 ● Goldeen
- ❑ 54/64 ● Jigglypuff
- ❑ 55/64 ● Mankey
- ❑ 56/64 ● Meowth
- ❑ 57/64 ● Nidoran ♀
- ❑ 58/64 ● Oddish
- ❑ 59/64 ● Paras
- ❑ 60/64 ● Pikachu
- ❑ 61/64 ● Rhyhorn
- ❑ 62/64 ● Spearow
- ❑ 63/64 ● Venonat
- ❑ 64/64 ● Poké Ball

FOSSIL

• • • • • • • • • • •

- ❑ 1/62 ★ Aerodactyl
- ❑ 2/62 ★ Articuno
- ❑ 3/62 ★ Ditto
- ❑ 4/62 ★ Dragonite
- ❑ 5/62 ★ Gengar
- ❑ 6/62 ★ Haunter
- ❑ 7/62 ★ Hitmonlee
- ❑ 8/62 ★ Hypno
- ❑ 9/62 ★ Kabutops
- ❑ 10/62 ★ Lapras
- ❑ 11/62 ★ Magneton
- ❑ 12/62 ★ Moltres
- ❑ 13/62 ★ Muk
- ❑ 14/62 ★ Raichu
- ❑ 15/62 ★ Zapdos

- ❑ 16/62 ★ Aerodactyl
- ❑ 17/62 ★ Articuno
- ❑ 18/62 ★ Ditto
- ❑ 19/62 ★ Dragonite
- ❑ 20/62 ★ Gengar
- ❑ 21/62 ★ Haunter
- ❑ 22/62 ★ Hitmonlee
- ❑ 23/62 ★ Hypno
- ❑ 24/62 ★ Kabutops
- ❑ 25/62 ★ Lapras
- ❑ 26/62 ★ Magneton
- ❑ 27/62 ★ Moltres
- ❑ 28/62 ★ Muk
- ❑ 29/62 ★ Raichu
- ❑ 30/62 ★ Zapdos
- ❑ 31/62 ◆ Arbok
- ❑ 32/62 ◆ Cloyster
- ❑ 33/62 ◆ Gastly
- ❑ 34/62 ◆ Golbat
- ❑ 35/62 ◆ Golduck
- ❑ 36/62 ◆ Golem
- ❑ 37/62 ◆ Graveler
- ❑ 38/62 ◆ Kingler
- ❑ 39/62 ◆ Magmar
- ❑ 40/62 ◆ Omastar
- ❑ 41/62 ◆ Sandslash
- ❑ 42/62 ◆ Seadra
- ❑ 43/62 ◆ Slowbro
- ❑ 44/62 ◆ Tentacruel
- ❑ 45/62 ◆ Weezing
- ❑ 46/62 ● Ekans
- ❑ 47/62 ● Geodude
- ❑ 48/62 ● Grimer
- ❑ 49/62 ● Horsea
- ❑ 50/62 ● Kabuto
- ❑ 51/62 ● Krabby
- ❑ 52/62 ● Omanyte

- ❑ 53/62 ● Psyduck
- ❑ 54/62 ● Shellder
- ❑ 55/62 ● Slowpoke
- ❑ 56/62 ● Tentacool
- ❑ 57/62 ● Zubat
- ❑ 58/62 ◆ Mr. Fuji
- ❑ 59/62 ● Energy Search
- ❑ 60/62 ● Gambler
- ❑ 61/62 ● Recycle
- ❑ 62/62 ● Mysterious Fossil

PROMOTIONAL CARDS

- ❑ 1 Pikachu
Pokémon TCG League
- ❑ 2 Electabuzz
Pokémon: The First Movie
- ❑ 3 Mewtwo
Pokémon: The First Movie
- ❑ 4 Pikachu
Pokémon: The First Movie
- ❑ 5 Dragonite
Pokémon: The First Movie
- ❑ 6 Arcanine
Pokémon TCG League
- ❑ 7 Jigglypuff
Pokémon: The First Movie Soundtrack
- ❑ 8 Mew
Pokémon TCG League

FREQUENTLY ASKED

QUESTIONS

• • • • • • • • • • • • • •

WE HAVE TO TRIED ANSWER a lot of your questions about how to play the **Pokémon** trading card game, how to collect cards and build decks, and, for you parents, how to manage the **Pokémon** phenomenon in your house.

But the chances are good that we didn't answer all of your questions. So, we went to our good friends at Wizards of the Coast Game Support (they're the people who answer our customer service phones and email lines) and we asked them: "What questions do you answer most often about the **Pokémon** TCG?"

In this chapter, we provide you with answers to the questions that our Game Support people (who answer thousands of **Pokémon** questions every day) are asked the most often. So if you have a question, it's very likely that you can find the answer here.

If you don't see your question answered here, you can always call Wizards of the Coast game support at 1-800-324-6496 or email them at questions@wizards.com and ask them directly.

PRODUCT QUESTIONS

Q: Why are Pokémon TCG cards so hard to find?

A: **Pokémon** TCG cards are so popular that the printing presses literally can't keep up with the demand for them. Don't worry though, Wizards of the Coast will continue to make as many **Pokémon** TCG cards available as possible.

Q: What should I do if my pack of Pokémon TCG cards doesn't contain the right number of cards, or the cards were damaged when I opened the pack?

A: If there's anything wrong with any **Pokémon** TCG products, be sure to save all the packaging and your receipt. Contact

TIP
You can ask the nice folks at Wizards of the Coast game support product and rules questions.

Wizards of the Coast game support. Do not send any cards to Wizards of the Coast unless a game support representative instructs you to.

Q: What's the difference between regular Pokémon TCG cards, *Jungle* cards, and *Fossil* cards?

A: The **Pokémon** trading card game has lots of different cards. Regular **Pokémon** TCG cards, *Jungle* cards, and *Fossil* cards are the same kind of cards. They all work together when you play the **Pokémon** TCG. The difference between each set is only that different cards are available. For instance, you can get Gengar only when you buy *Fossil.* You can use cards from the Base Set (the official term for the first "regular" set of **Pokémon** TCG cards), Base Set 2 (the new "regular" set that replaces Base Set and includes some cards from the *Jungle* set), and any expansions together in the same deck.

Q: I thought I had every Pokémon TCG card, but then I saw a 1st Edition version of Raichu. Are

 there any cards that are only available in the 1st Edition?

A: Cards with the 1st Edition symbol are the same as cards without the 1st Edition symbol in every way except for this additional symbol. There are no cards that are only available in 1st Edition version. Just like there are 130 different Base Set 2 cards, there are

130 Base Set 2 cards with the 1st Edition symbol. There aren't 260 different Base Set 2 cards.

Cards with the 1st Edition symbol are printed in limited quantities. Once they're sold out, no more will ever be made. All further versions of those cards are identical, except for the 1st Edition symbol.

Q: How do I tell if a Pokémon TCG card is real or fake?

A: There are a few ways you can tell if a **Pokémon** card is a fake. Some fake cards are smaller than real **Pokémon** TCG cards, and you can tell right away by placing the card you are worried about on top of a real card. If they aren't the same size, then the card in question is a fake. Some fake cards are just stickers stuck onto real **Pokémon** TCG cards. These cards will be thicker and stiffer than real **Pokémon** TCG cards.

You can also use the "light test." Hold the card up to a light. If you can see the light through the card, then it is a fake. Because the paper stock on some counterfeit cards is thinner, they feel lighter, bend more easily, and allow light to shine through. You should also check the legal text at the

TIP
Can you see light through your **Pokémon** card? Is the red side of the Poké Ball on the back facing the bottom of the card? You have a fake card!

bottom of the card. If the legal text is blurry or doesn't appear at all, the card is a fake.

GAME PLAY QUESTIONS

Q: **At the beginning of a game, how do you decide who shows their hand first if both players have no Basic Pokémon in their first seven cards?**

A: You should flip a coin to see who will go first before you and your opponent draw your first seven cards. Let's say Susie wins the coin flip. Since Susie will go first in the game, she will also be the first person to reveal her hand if she has no Basic Pokémon. Each time Susie draws a new hand of seven cards, her opponent, Evan, may draw two additional cards.

Once Susie is done drawing a new hand of seven cards, Evan checks all the cards in his hand for Basic Pokémon, not just his first seven cards. If Evan still doesn't have any Basic Pokémon, he has to shuffle all the cards back into his deck and draw a new hand of seven cards. Susie may draw two cards each time Evan does this.

Q: **I learned how to play the Pokémon TCG with only three Prizes, but my friend tells me we're supposed to play with six. Who's right?**

A: You probably learned how to play the **Pokémon** TCG from the Starter Set, which comes with two 30-card decks and has you play a shorter, 3-Prize game. Starter Sets are designed to teach you how to play the **Pokémon** TCG quickly. They use special rules to do so, including smaller decks and fewer Prizes. In a real game of the **Pokémon** TCG, you play with 60-card decks and deal out six Prizes at the beginning of the game.

Q: **Can I discard Energy cards from my hand to retreat my Active Pokémon?**

A: Energy cards used to pay for your Pokémon's Retreat Cost must be ones attached to the Pokémon.

Q: **When I Knock Out one of my opponent's Pokémon, I take one of his Prize cards, right?**

A: No. You never take any of your opponent's cards or give up any of your own cards in a game. When you Knock Out an opponent's Pokémon, you take one of *your* Prizes and put it in your hand. When you draw your last Prize, you win!

Q: **If I have a Pokémon with only 10 points of damage, can I use the Potion Trainer card to heal it, or does the Pokémon need to have at least 20 damage before I can play the Potion?**

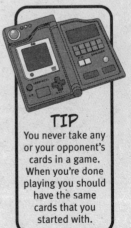

TIP
You never take any or your opponent's cards in a game. When you're done playing you should have the same cards that you started with.

A: Potion says, "Remove up to 2 damage counters from one of your Pokémon." If you want to play that card on a Pokémon that has only one damage counter, you can. You don't have to wait until the Pokémon actually has 20 or more damage before you can play the card.

Q: **What about Professor Oak? That card says, "Discard your hand, then draw 7 cards." Can I play Professor Oak if I don't have any cards in my hand? What if I don't have seven cards left in my deck?**

A: When you play Professor Oak, you don't need to have any cards in your hand. You always have a hand, even if there are no cards in it. So, you simply discard your hand of zero cards. Other cards, such as Energy Retrieval, say, "trade 1 of the other cards in your hand for up to 2 basic Energy cards from your discard pile." So to play Energy Retrieval, you have to have another card *in your hand*.

If you don't have seven cards left in your deck, you can still play Professor Oak. When a card tells you to do something like, "draw 7 cards," you keep drawing cards until you either have drawn 7 cards, or you can't draw any more cards. Don't worry, you won't lose the game because you played Professor Oak. The only time you lose the game because you can't draw a card is at the beginning of your turn.

Q: **Are Pokémon Powers always on or do you have to declare when you are using them? Can you use them from the Bench?**

A: Pokémon Powers can be used by any Pokémon in play (Benched Pokémon are in play too). Many Pokémon Powers must be used before you attack. Others work all the time. A few only work when something else happens. Each Pokémon Power is different, though, so you should read them carefully to see how they work.

If the card text for a Pokémon Power doesn't say you have a choice, it's always on. For example, Omanyte's Pokémon Power: Clairvoyance says, "Your opponent plays with his or her hand face up."

If a Pokémon Power uses the word "may" that usually means you have to declare when you're using it. For instance, Gengar's Pokémon Power: Curse says, "Once during your turn (before you attack), you may move 1 damage counter from 1 of your opponent's Pokémon to another *(even if it would Knock Out the other Pokémon)."*

If a Pokémon Power uses

TIP
Pokémon Powers can be used by any Pokémon in play, even benched ones!

the word "whenever," it works only when something else happens. For example, Machamp's Pokémon Power: Strikes Back says, "Whenever your opponent's attack damages Machamp, this power does 10 damage to the attacking Pokémon."

Q: How do you tell whether something is a cost or an effect?

A: When a Pokémon's text or a Trainer card tells you to do something, that's an effect. For instance, Bulbasaur's Leech Seed attack says, "Unless all damage from this attack is prevented, you may remove 1 damage counter from Bulbasaur." That means that whenever Bulbasaur uses Leech Seed, you get to remove one damage counter from it (unless all that damage was prevented). Removing the damage counter is an effect.

When a card tells you to do something in order to use a Pokémon's attack or Trainer card, that something is a cost. You must be able to do that something if you want to use that attack or play that Trainer card. For instance, Charmander's Ember says, "Discard 1 Fire Energy card attached to Charmander *in order to* use this attack."

Q: Alakazam's Pokémon Power: Damage Swap says, "you may move 1 damage counter from 1

of your Pokémon to another as long as you don't Knock Out that Pokémon." Can I use this Pokémon Power to move damage counters from my Pokémon to my opponent's Pokémon?

A: Damage Swap only lets you move damage counters from one of your Pokémon to another *of your* Pokémon. You can't use Damage Swap to move damage counters from your Pokémon to your opponent's Pokémon.

> **TIP**
> If you have any questions about the **Pokémon** TCG, call Wizards of the Coast game support at 1-800-324-6496!

NEED MORE INFORMATION?

To find a Pokémon TCG League Center:
Look for one of the locations listed in this book or follow the League link at www.wizards.com/pokemon.

For general product and rules questions about the Pokémon TCG:
Contact Wizards of the Coast Game Support.
Call 1-800-324-6496 or email questions@wizards.com

CHECK OUT THESE UPCOMING BOOKS:

Team Rocket Strategy Guide
• Every card shown; card tips and tricks, deck ideas; special *Fossil* section

Let's Play Pokémon: The Ultimate Guide for Parents and Kids
• Full color guide; play, trade, and deck building tips; more activities for parents and kids